TWICE UPON A TIME

Rapunzel

The One with All the Hair

WENDY MASS

SCHOLASTIC INC.

*To Norman and Adaya for the Florida sun;
and to Lisa, Gail, Betsy, and Pat for helping
Rapunzel's hair to grow*

Copyright © 2006 by Wendy Mass

All rights reserved. Published by Scholastic Inc., *Publishers since 1920.* SCHOLASTIC and associated logos are trademarks and/or registered trademarks of Scholastic Inc.

The publisher does not have any control over and does not assume any responsibility for author or third-party websites or their content.

No part of this publication may be reproduced, stored in a retrieval system, or transmitted in any form or by any means, electronic, mechanical, photocopying, recording, or otherwise, without written permission of the publisher. For information regarding permission, write to Scholastic Inc., Attention: Permissions Department, 557 Broadway, New York, NY 10012.

This book is a work of fiction. Names, characters, places, and incidents are either the product of the author's imagination or are used fictitiously, and any resemblance to actual persons, living or dead, business establishments, events, or locales is entirely coincidental.

ISBN 978-0-439-79659-0

10 9 8 7 6 5 4 3 2 1   17 18 19 20 21

Printed in the U.S.A.   40
First printing 2017

CHAPTER ONE

∽ Rapunzel ∾

5th of Augustus

I seriously CANNOT BELIEVE what has happened to me today. I am currently throwing a tantrum on the pile of straw that is supposed to serve as my bed (!) and — this is the most unbelievable part — I am LOCKED IN A TOWER IN THE MIDDLE OF THE FOREST!! In case I am never rescued and blackbirds fly through the one tower window and pick my bones clean, I hope the tragic circumstances that have befallen me on the dawn of my twelfth birthday will not go forgotten by history. Kicking and screaming in frustration is not doing me much good. Truth be told, my body is beginning to ache from the effort.

My candle sheds just enough light for me to see the strange shadows dancing on the walls. The only reason I am not lying in complete darkness is that the witch (yes, WITCH, complete with scraggly hair and hairy wart) did not know a handful of candles was in the trunk along with the meager possessions she allowed me to pack.

My day started out fine. Mother was preparing a special

morning feast to celebrate my birthday, and I was setting up the stool and shears that she was going to use later to cut my hair. Now that I turned twelve, this was to be my first official haircut and I couldn't wait. Once it was shortened, I could finally wear my hair loose instead of tied upon my head. It was so long I could sit on it!

From the kitchen window, I could see Father out back, tending the garden. He is famous in our village for the rampion herb that refuses to grow in any yard but ours. In the heat of summer, the orders for fresh rampion pour in and we live high off the hog (or herb, as the case may be) right through the autumn harvest. Then, in November, I help Father dig up the stalks and he rides off for a fortnight to deliver the herb as far as the riverbank on the other side of the Great Forest.

Some ladies boil it and apply it to their cheeks for a smooth complexion. Mostly, though, it is made into salads along with lettuce and spinach. I've heard whispers that there's something not natural about rampion, that it can make feeble old men strong again and will keep your breath fresh even if you bite into a clove of garlic.

Mother had finished spreading honey on the almond pies that would be my special birthday breakfast, and told me to go fetch Father. When I pushed open the heavy wooden gate that protected the garden, I was shocked to see that Father was not alone. In twelve years of life, I had never seen an outsider in the garden. The stranger wore a black cape with a hood, even though it was deadly hot out. I could not tell whether it was a man or a woman, only that he or she wasn't much taller than I.

Father and the stranger looked to be in heated debate. I dared not move closer lest the bells on my belt alert them to my presence. Soon the gate behind me banged open and Mother appeared. I could tell she was about to scold me for dawdling when her eyes lit upon the stranger. Her hands flew to her mouth. She gasped, and the sound caught their attention. The stranger turned and I saw immediately that it was an old woman with beady, penetrating black eyes, white hair, and a long nose. Three large flies circled around her head but she did not wave them away. I felt a cold shiver run down my spine.

Mother grabbed the sleeve of my special yellow birthday dress and tried to pull me back into the house. It was no use. Our feet were suddenly stuck to the ground. Mother started to cry. Father buried his face in his hands. I was too shocked to do either of those things; I just gaped at the woman.

She crept toward me. "You must be Rapunzel," she said in a raspy voice. "I've waited a long time for you."

Father rushed over and stood between us. "You cannot

have her," he said firmly. "We made that deal before she was born. Surely you cannot hold us to it."

Mother paused from her crying to yell at Father. "It was not WE. It was YOU! YOU made that deal!"

Father yelled back, "You wouldn't eat anything other than the witch's rampion! After we prayed for a baby for all those years, I couldn't very well let you starve when you needed your strength for the birth!"

I turned my head between the two of them. Mother pursed her lips and didn't respond. A *witch*?! A birth? Did they mean *me*? I managed to make my mouth work enough to ask my parents, "Will someone tell *me* what is going on? Who is this . . . this *person*?"

The old woman made a loud cackling sound. I think it was a laugh.

"Stupid man," she said to Father in a dark whisper, "you don't make a bargain with a witch and expect her not to hold you to it. Our deal was clear: your freedom for your daughter. You stole the rampion from my garden, and I did not destroy you for your thievery. I've made you a rich man all these years. Now that she is a maiden, I have come for her."

She *did* mean me! My eyes widened. The old lady grinned and her wart stretched along with her lips. Don't even ask me to describe her teeth, because what was left of them was not pretty. She must be a rather poor witch if she can't even fix her own appearance. I mean, honestly, even the apothecary in town can cure a wart.

Things happened quickly after that. My father picked me up in his arms (and I'm no little thing anymore) and tried to run. He, too, found that his legs refused to move. With a swoosh of the witch's arm, all the green stalks in the garden fell to the ground and shriveled up like they'd never sprouted at all. With alarming physical strength, the witch pulled me from my father's arms and dragged me into the house. Mother's shrieks followed us. The witch seemed to know where my room was, because she led me straight to it and ordered me to pack my bare necessities in the wooden chest. I tried to dart from the room but she blocked the door. Then I did as she instructed . . . because what else could I do? I grabbed what I could until she slammed the chest shut.

In an instant I was blindfolded and found myself lying across the seat of a swiftly moving carriage. I tried to scream but my voice had left me. Being familiar with the pathways of the village, I tried to follow the turns of the streets but soon was lost. I felt very drowsy and had to fight to keep my wits about me.

The next thing I knew, I awoke on a pile of straw. The blindfold now off, I could see in the fading daylight that I was in a round room, with a threadbare blue rug covering the center of the stone floor. Faded as it was, the rug provided the only splash of color in the place. The walls were built of gray rectangular stones that did not let in even the tiniest crack of daylight. Even in the height of summer, the room had a cold dampness to it. My eyes lit upon an open window, big enough for me to climb out of. I couldn't believe my luck! I ran up to it and was about to swing one leg over the ledge when I saw what was below me. The treetops! I stared in awe. I'd never seen the tops of the trees before.

I realized with a sickening feeling that I was higher than the tallest spire in the village. I stuck my head out and looked down. It was dizzying. There were stones all the way down — no other windows, no doors or ladders that I could see. I figured the tower was about twenty times taller than me, and I'm tall for my age. A party of blackbirds was lazily circling the tower, cawing occasionally. Their presence did not inspire confidence. Were not blackbirds the ones who waited for people and animals to die and then picked over their remains? Or maybe those were ravens. I did not want to find out.

I backed away from the window and moved along the walls, feeling carefully for loose stones or the outline of a door. There were none. I lifted the dusty rug. No trapdoor in the floor. The only other objects in the room besides the straw "bed" and my trunk were a small table and chair that looked like they may have once been painted but were now a dull gray. When I stood perfectly still in the center of the room, I could have sworn I heard a rhythmic breathing, but I was clearly alone.

Now, utterly exhausted from the events of the day, I lie here and wonder: How did I get in here if no door is to be found? How will I get out? What will become of me? Are there ghosts of other young girls in here, also forced away from their parents and their homes?

My first pimple is upon me from all the stress.

CHAPTER TWO

← Prince Benjamin →

5ᵗʰ *of Augustus*

A prince's life is not as exciting as one might imagine. So far I have had no grand adventures. Certainly nothing that a traveling minstrel would write a song about. For instance, this morning I practiced my backstroke in the castle pond and watched enviously as the squires jousted in the nearby fields. At night I dream of becoming a knight, but that is not my destiny. I shall be a king someday. That's simply the way it works.

After swimming, I tried but failed to locate where I had last set my extra pair of glasses. My mother, the queen — or Mum, as I call her — gets vexed when I do not have them at hand. She is always worried I'll lose the ones tied with horsehair around my neck and walk into a wall or fall down the dung chute straight into the moat. I am quite blind without them.

Mum watches me like a hawk. My father, the king, says it is not good for a woman to baby her thirteen-year-old son. I couldn't agree more. She won't even let me listen to the fiddlers who practice in the courtyard. I'm lucky if they don't make me leave when the minstrel plays at supper on Sundays. She says it is not healthy for a boy of my position to be so enthralled by music, so she took away my lute when I was nine. She'd rather I practice my discus throwing or archery, but I'm so uncoordinated that I tend to shoot my arrows too close to unsuspecting couples out for a stroll in the gardens.

Swimming is about the only physical activity during which I am unlikely to injure anyone. I am also good at chess, which I feel should count as physical activity because you have to reach over and move pieces all the time. Some of the boards are quite large, so one must lean AND reach at the same time, thereby expending even more energy. Mum does not agree that chess equals physical activity, and thus I am only allowed to play on Sundays.

Fortunately for all of us, Mum has a real baby to baby, my sister Annabelle, who is three years of age. Annabelle smells quite poor due to the fact that she refuses to be trained to use the dung chute, but she is bubbly and sweet. Truth be told, I am quite fond of her.

Andrew, my favorite page and my only real confidante in the castle, has come to fetch me for supper in the Great Hall, where I will be made to sit next to Prince Elkin, the ever-bothersome, froglike cousin of mine who is visiting for the summer. I will have to pretend that I cannot see the rye seeds stuck in his teeth or his unnaturally round bug-eyes. He is a year my elder but is so short that it is hard to remember that I am the younger. I will be on my best behavior. That is what princes do.

Mostly.

EVENING

I have been sent to my room by Father. Apparently I am still not old enough to join the lords and ladies who have gathered to watch the court jester dance, joke-tell, and juggle three silver balls. They will drink ale and brandy, and laugh at the jester in the floppy hat who, if you want my honest opinion, looks very silly for a grown man in that silver-and-purple silk outfit.

Still, I'd like to be able to watch. The worst part is that Elkin (who, as I suspected, has rye seeds and parsley stuck in his teeth) is up here in my room with me. I am planning to ignore him by reading my favorite book and sulking. It truly burns me up. At my age, some princes are already *married* and can listen to wandering minstrels and jesters whenever they please! Not that I would ever want that fate, mind you. Girls my age make me uneasy. I was asked to leave the winter ball last year when I caused a princess's foot to bleed from stepping on it so many times. In my own defense, I have recently had a growth spurt that has left me tall and gangly. I am waiting impatiently for the return of the balance that I once had in my childhood.

"Stop," Elkin says, putting his hand on my arm as I reach for *The Adventures of Roland, the Great Knight,* which has a permanent spot on my bedside table. "What are you doing?"

"If you must know, I am going to find out how Roland rescues the damsel in distress." Reading is my favorite pastime, and if I were not a prince destined one day to be a king, I would be an illuminator who paints wondrous pictures in books. If I couldn't be a knight, that is.

"There. Is. A. JESTER. Downstairs," Elkin says slowly, as though I don't speak the language.

"Yes, Elkin, I am aware. That is why we have been sent to my room." This boy is truly daft.

"Then why are we dawdling here?" he asks, grabbing hold of my arm and tugging me toward the door. "Let us be off to the sitting room!"

I must say, I am surprised at his boldness. As much as I would like to do as he suggests because the call to adventure is very great in me, I pull away. "We can't go down there; Father does not like being disobeyed. It's a king thing — you know how it is. Can't show weakness, and all that."

"Then we shall hide behind the couch and they will be

none the wiser. Do come, Benjamin. I've never seen a jester before." His cheeks are glowing with excitement, making his carrot-colored hair look even brighter than usual.

It *is* temping. "But if we hide behind the couch, we will not be able to see the jester. What would be the point?"

"At least we could hear him," Elkin says pleadingly. "Now come!"

Elkin is more forceful than I had imagined. I suppose the adventures of Roland can wait. I follow Elkin out the door and down the tapestry-lined hallway. I feel that the great knights and ladies in the wall hangings are watching us with disapproval.

We make it to the sitting room without getting caught. Which is a miracle, really, on account of all the servants and maids running hither and yon. I follow Elkin behind the largest of the velvet couches and we wait for the adults to come in. We don't have long to wait. We have just tucked our feet underneath us when the room begins to fill. Mum sits down right in front of me, with Annabelle on her lap. Apparently Annabelle is allowed to be here because she won't understand the jester's sense of humor. Harumph.

Everything is going according to plan. The jester makes his entrance and the audience's clapping echoes loudly in the cavernous room. If it were not the start of Augustus, it would be very cold on this floor and I should be much less comfortable. The jester must have begun his performance by juggling, because the adults are oohing and aahing without his saying a word. Then I hear, "And this pretty little silver apple is for the pretty little lady." He must be handing something to my sister because she squeals and says, "Wheeee! Apull!" Then she must try to bite it, because Mum says, "No, dear babe, that is not dessert."

One of the lords sitting by the window chimes in with, "Let us hope she stays as pretty come her marriage day a decade hence."

Mum laughs nervously. "Of course she will, Lord Albrick. You have nothing to worry about."

What is that? What is she saying? She's marrying off my sister a decade hence, when she is *my* age? My three-year-old sister is *engaged*? I start to stand in protest when Elkin grabs me and forces me back down. My glasses nearly fly off my face.

"It is not for myself that I worry," Lord Albrick replies. "My boy is quite picky, you know. He is only seven now, but already he can tell if a lady's hair is not properly combed and bound."

My blood is starting to boil. My father clears his throat and says, "I assure you that my daughter, the *princess*, will not disappoint."

Annabelle chooses this moment to yell out, "Poopy bottom, poopy poo!"

Elkin and I stifle our laughter. Too bad Lord Albrick's picky son couldn't hear his future bride now! Mum hushes her, and the jester begins to sing a little ditty about a knight rescuing a fair maiden.

Darn the stupid tradition of marrying off children so two families can merge their assets and increase their status. My father has been trying to annex Lord Albrick's estate for years now. Clearly he's found the way to do it — by promising my sweet baby sister to some bratty kid!

Since there is nothing I can do about it now, I must try to relax and listen to the jester's song. He is singing about a great knight riding out at dawn on his trusty steed in search of a missing princess. I am wondering why princesses always go missing, when I notice that my friend Andrew, the page, has come into the room with a tray of mead. He is about to hand one to Mum when he catches sight of us. (Elkin's hair practically *glows*, and is thus very eye-catching). I put my finger to my lips, but it is already too late. In his surprise, Andrew lets the goblet slip out of his hand. Mead spills onto Mum's lap (and, therefore, Annabelle's lap), the goblet crashes to the floor, the jester stops jesting, the knight stops rescuing, and Elkin and I are caught red-handed (or red-haired, as the case may be).

We guiltily get to our feet while Andrew and the maids scramble to clean Mum and Annabelle. Mum does not look happy to be pawed at by three different maids and a page. Poor Andrew. He was never very fond of Elkin (who is, really?) but I know he feels bad for unwittingly blowing our cover. I must admit, it is nice having someone else be the cause of a spill now and again. Usually it is my own clumsiness that causes people to have to change their clothes.

"That's quite enough," Mum says, holding up her hand. "I shall retire to my chambers for the night. The hour has grown late." She shakes her head meaningfully at Elkin and me, and we shrink back toward the wall. She lifts Annabelle onto one hip, picks up her skirts with her free hand, and swooshes out of the room. Then everyone turns their attention back to us. Even the jester is glaring, which truly does not seem necessary. After all, it was not we who spilled the wine. Well, not directly.

"Explain," Father says, his deep voice rumbling. He is a king of few words.

Elkin and I exchange quick glances. This is the part where he would usually blame it all on me, like the time we were ten and got caught putting a live eel in the cook's lunch sack. Elkin claimed it was all my idea — which it was NOT — and I was made to sweep the floors in the dining room for a week. The cook boiled up the eel and served it for dinner, so no harm was truly done. Except, perhaps, to the eel.

But now Elkin surprises me and says, "Forgive me, uncle. It was my fault. Benjamin did not want to disobey you."

I could not be more surprised if I had just heard that I was going to be allowed to be a knight after all. Father looks from one of us to the other, thoughtfully. Father believes a good ruler never blurts out what he is thinking without fully weighing it from all angles.

I am banished to my room (again), alone this time. Father has decided that Elkin is not a good influence on me.

I would turn to the adventures of Roland the Great Knight for comfort, but my book has been taken away from me in punishment. Annabelle runs into my room on her short little legs, flings herself onto the bed, stands and jumps off the bed, then runs out. All without saying a word.

How I long for the innocence of youth.

CHAPTER THREE

∽ Rapunzel ∾

6th of Augustus

I have been crying and am not ashamed to admit it. I miss my parents even though they traded me for a stinking herb. (Literally, it stinks. Sometimes I can't get it out of my dresses for weeks, no matter how hard I rub.)

I am hungry and my bones ache from the miserable sleeping arrangements. I need to get hold of myself. I decide to take inventory of supplies. This is what I own:

1 wooden chest
1 scratchy wool blanket that was left on the straw "bed"
3 pink ribbons for my hair
4 beeswax candles and 20 wooden matches
1 sheepskin belt with 6 tiny bells strung on it
5 dresses
3 pieces of vellum with which to record my last will and
     testament
1 goose quill to write with and a pot of ink that,
     thankfully, did not spill in transport

2 white feathers that have wafted in through the
   window
1 pair of leather-soled boots
1 small mirror (in which I can see my pimple growing by
   the second)
1 metal comb
1 tin of healing ointment that Mother concocted from
   last season's rampion harvest. (I am tempted to
   throw this out the window.)
1 shawl that used to be in my infant crib. Mother knit it
   for me.

And that's all. That's everything I have to my name.

I weep some more. When I am done and have wiped my
eyes, I suddenly notice a silver plate piled high with food
sitting in the center of the rug. Was it there this whole morning? I circle around the food a few times before picking up
the plate and taking it to the small table. Ground mutton
and onions. Not my normal breakfast, but nothing is normal anymore.

Once the food is in my belly, I begin to feel better. I'm
sure my parents will come for me today. The witch has made
her point. How long could she really keep me a prisoner?
My father has some stature in the village. She can't get away
with kidnapping me for long. I am sure of it.

EVENING

I am no longer sure of anything. It is dark and stuffy in here. I am alone (except for the ghostly breathing that I swear I still hear but am trying valiantly to ignore). I have lit another candle, but it is burning quickly and I have only three left. My hair hurts. I hadn't known that hair could hurt, but it does. I will soon develop a headache. Normally my mother would have unpinned it from my head and brushed it out after supper. If yesterday had gone as it was supposed to, I wouldn't have all this hair anymore. It would be a sensible length, perhaps gently gracing my shoulders.

My tears have run dry. I shall cry no more for now.

LATER THAT EVENING

I hear a scurrying sound like fingernails skittering along the stone floor. I am curled up in a very small ball and have buried my head under my shawl. It smells faintly of Mother's scent. And — ugh — of rampion.

CHAPTER FOUR

← Prince Benjamin →

6th of Augustus

My punishment has been lifted. Mum has a soft spot for me, her only son, the future king. I might as well have stayed in bed, though, because today was very annoying. This is what I did:

1. Fished for eels in the pond with Elkin and was tempted to push him into the water, but did not since, after all, he told the truth for once when we got caught behind the couch.
2. Chased a hare across the banks, then felt guilty. Felt wimpy for feeling guilty and chased it some more.
3. Discovered a new pimple growing on my forehead. Covered it with my hair until Mum told me that I looked like a tall brown mop and pushed it back to its proper position. Elkin laughed and pointed at the red spot. He is quickly losing any ground he may have gained last night.

After supper, I chewed some fresh mint and sage to lessen the pimple's swelling. The herbs might have been rancid, because my belly aches now. Or perhaps I am being punished for chasing the hare. I shall try to find him tomorrow to apologize. I am retiring early tonight with *The Adventures of Roland* to keep me company.

CHAPTER FIVE

⊷ Prince Benjamin ⊶
7th of Augustus

Elkin is going home early! My aunt is coming to fetch him today. He was supposed to stay all summer, but it turns out Elkin is to be engaged to a princess from a neighboring kingdom! Mum made the announcement at breakfast this morning. Elkin turned pale, causing his freckles to stand out even more. I choked on my bread and had to be smacked on the back by the closest serving maid. When I was done choking, I asked, "Is his wife three years old?"

Mum shot me a disapproving look. "The young lady is of suitable age, I assure you both."

Elkin's normally buggy eyes were huge then. He asked gravely, "When is this marriage due to take place?"

Mum laughed. "Not for a few years, child. Your days of mischief aren't over quite yet."

Elkin let out a huge breath. "Thank goodness!"

After breakfast, Elkin went to his bedchambers to pack and I went into the sitting room and did a little jig. (When no one is around to make me nervous, I am not nearly as clumsy.)

Now I am sitting on a bench outside, watching the falconer train the hawks on the Great Lawn. I hear the pounding of horses' hooves on the rocky path before I see them. A moment later, the royal courier announces the arrival of my aunt's gilded carriage. Their kingdom is not as grand as ours, but even as a lower queen, my aunt travels in style, accompanied by squires and archers on horseback.

Elkin comes to the front door and I rise to shake his hand. His face is pale and sweaty. He actually looks quite ill. If it were me, Mum would have me in bed with the doctor at my side. My aunt does not even emerge from the carriage. She merely raises her hand in greeting. Elkin turns to wave at me again before a young page lifts his bags into the carriage and gently closes the door. I wave back and feel a tad guilty for not being nicer to him. I hope he will be happy with his future bride and that they will have many redheaded children. May blessings be upon their heads.

I am off to find my hare.

CHAPTER SIX

∽ Rapunzel ∾

7th of Augustus

The tears have started again even though I told myself that I am too old to cry like a swaddled babe. I am unable to make myself leave this scratchy pile of straw. I couldn't even eat the plate of porridge and cheese that magically appeared again this morning. The witch has not shown her warty face since my imprisonment began. Oh, how I wish this were no more than a bad dream. Yes, of course! I'm sure that it is nothing more than a passing nightmare! How could I have thought that my parents — my darling, loving, sweet, kind parents — would have promised me to a witch in exchange for a salad ingredient? Absurd! I bet if I take a little nap, I will awaken in my own bed, atop my soft feather mattress, my cat Pumpkin warming my feet. Good night!

EVENING

When I awake from my nap some hours later, I do not open my eyes at first. I lie still until I am sure. Yes! There is definitely a warm body on my feet! And a purring! I am

HOME!! My eyes fly open only to find I am most certainly NOT home. Curiously, though, there actually IS a cat on my feet! I rub my eyes and look again. She is small and orange, a kitten not much bigger than my foot. She must have been responsible for the scratching and scurrying that I heard last night, and hopefully the rhythmic breathing as well. I shall name her Sir Kitty.

I admit I have cheered since her arrival. I know not how she got in, or where she was hiding, but I am very pleased for her company. It is quite comforting to have another living creature in here. The sun is setting through my small window, so the day is almost spent. No parents have come. The plate of food that I ignored this morning has been taken away. I wish I had forced myself to eat, because my belly is rumbling. I recall Mother saying once that time moves more quickly for busy people. I must find some way to pass the time until the breakfast meal tomorrow. For one thing, I can undo my hair, which has become a big scraggly mess. I will soon look like a witch myself if I don't do something!

It takes me a good half hour to pull all the pins out of my hair. I add them to my list of possessions and place them carefully in my trunk. When my hair is finally free, I shake it out and run the comb through it. Or, I should say, I TRY to run the comb through it. Mother would weep to see me right now. By the time I finally get all the tangles out, the sun has set. I light the candle and melt the bottom so it stands upright on the small wooden table. I realize with a start that my hair reaches almost to my feet! Sir Kitty meows in delight and tries to climb it.

"Ow! Stop that, Sir Kitty! It hurts!"

"Does it now?" a voice asks, sounding amused. "We wouldn't want you in any discomfort."

I whirl around and find the witch standing on the rug in the center of the room.

"Where did . . . how did . . . where —" I can't seem to get the words out. Sir Kitty burrows under my hair and starts to quiver.

"It is of no importance to you where I came from," she says, taking a step toward me.

I open my mouth to beg to differ, but one look from her and I close it. She sets a plate of steaming food on the table next to my candle. I don't want to take my eyes off her, but I can't stop ogling the roast pig with a side of peas and carrots. The tea in the copper mug looks crisp and refreshing. But I cannot let myself be distracted! I put my hands on my hips and try to look fierce.

"Now look here, witch," I say in my most imposing voice — which, let's face it, isn't very imposing at all. "My parents will be here any minute. You might as well let me out of here right now or . . . or . . . you will face the hang-man's noose for sure!" I stamp my foot for emphasis.

For a moment, she doesn't say anything; she just looks at me, surprised. I must have scared her into realizing what she did was very wrong. I begin to fantasize about what I shall do first thing when I get home. Well, I shall bathe, of course, and eat the almond birthday pie that I never got a chance to enjoy. And after that, I'll —

Suddenly the witch starts laughing. She laughs so hard, she actually clutches her belly. Then she throws back her head and guffaws some more. Finally she stops, wipes some tears from her craggy face, and says, "Ah, foolish girl. Foolish Rapunzel, the name I gave you twelve short years ago. Your parents are not looking for you, and no one will ever find you here. We are far, far away from any village or riding path. Quite well hidden. The only visitors you shall have are the birds and the flies. And me, of course. You may call me Mother Gothel. You and I will become great friends."

Then she laughs again and I recoil, almost knocking over the table with all the food on it. What does she mean that she named me? Mother told me my godmother named me Rapunzel after her favorite food. Wait a moment! I recall the schoolmaster taught us that *rapunzel* was another name for rampion! Will I NEVER be free of that herb? I am starting to realize that Mother may have lied about a thing or two. If I ever get out of here, she and I are going to have some words.

I wish the witch would leave already so I might dine in peace. Instead, she reaches out and touches my hair. I want to scream, but I will not give her the satisfaction of showing my fright. She strokes it softly. "I see you have let down your hair, child. It has grown since your birth, yes?" She curls her fist around a section, then lets it slip through her fingers.

"Yes, well, Mother was supposed to cut it on my birthday, but I was rudely and savagely kidnapped before she had a chance."

The witch raises one eyebrow, and half of her mouth twitches. As a result, she looks half amused and half furious. She orders me to stand facing the window like an obedient child. I start to protest, but her eyes darken. I pick up Sir Kitty and place her on the "bed." The witch watches me very closely.

"Where did that animal come from?" she hisses.

I keep my back to her and hope she doesn't hear how hard my heart has started to beat. I don't know what I would do if she took away Sir Kitty. "It must have been hiding here the whole time, witch." I keep one hand on the kitten protectively.

"I told you to call me Mother Gothel! Now go to the

window! Do not turn around until you have braided that hair of yours. You are too old to be walking around with a mop like that!"

"I know that!" I say, turning to face her. "I told you it was already supposed to be cut!"

She points to the window. The conversation is apparently over. I don't tell her that I have never braided my own hair. Mother has always done it. I am afraid if I tell her, she might do it herself, and the thought of her touching me again makes me shudder. I have braided rope before, so perhaps it is not that different.

I face the window and gather my thick hair away from my face like Mother used to do. Using both hands, I reach around the back of my head. It takes me a good twenty minutes to make a braid that feels something like what Mother used to make. When I am done, my arms ache. I rest my hands on the ledge and find that if I lean slightly forward, I can catch the light breeze that comes off the treetops. The moon hangs low in the sky, illuminating the forest. It does not shed much light into the tower, though. Perhaps my parents are looking up now, too, and wondering where their only child has been taken. I still believe they will come for me. Surely they will leave no stone unturned, no tower unsearched. The witch said I could turn around after I completed the braid, but I'd rather look at the night than her

face. After a minute, though, I hear a crunching and scratching behind me. What is the witch doing now?? I sneak a
peek over my shoulder. To my relief, the witch is gone,
simply vanished. And Sir Kitty is happily munching on my
roast pig!

CHAPTER SEVEN

⊹ Prince Benjamin ⊹
7ᵗʰ *of Augustus*

Normally I would not be allowed to wander the grounds unattended, but today Mum was busy sulking because her sister did not deem it necessary to come in to visit when she picked up Elkin. Mum is convinced that her sister has never forgiven her for marrying the better king. She spent the day holed up with the seamstress and embroiderer, who together are making her a new wardrobe. This always makes her feel better.

This is what I learned on my journey to ask forgiveness from the hare:

1. All hares look the same.
2. If you pick a hare that you think could have been your hare, in that it has the same patch of brown on its rump as the one you chased, and if you bend down to talk to it, and if it then blinks at you and hops off, the peasant children who live on the outskirts of the castle grounds will look at you strangely.

3. When the peasant children look at you strangely, and you cross your eyes at them and wag your tongue a little, they will laugh and run off, proving that you are good with children.
4. Peasants live very differently from those of us in the castle.

Certainly I have been aware for many years that the peasants don't have the same luxuries my family does, but until today, I had never actually been inside one of their homes. There are dozens of young people living within a mile of the castle gates, yet I call none friend. Even Andrew is more of a secret friend since we are not of the same social stature. We loan each other books and sneak down into the kitchen at midnight for leftover plum cakes. He reads as much as he can, for he will become a squire soon and then a knight one day, with not much time for books.

My father is a generous king, and no one goes hungry in his kingdom. Still, the home that I visited did not have much by way of comforts. No thick velvet couches. No serving staff of twenty. The pigs and chickens wandered in and out of the house as though it were the most natural thing.

When my hare had hopped away (I'm beginning to doubt that it *was* mine after all) and I crossed my eyes and wagged my tongue, I was perhaps a bit overzealous, because as I danced about, my glasses fell to the ground. They were not the ones attached to the horsehair chain, because those have gone missing. (It was only a matter of time until they did. Truly, I lose my glasses with remarkable swiftness. This is my last pair and the merchant who sells them will not be at the castle till next winter.) When I dropped to my knees to feel around for them, I discovered they had broken right down the middle section that normally sits on the bridge of my nose. The only way I could see even a little was to hold one lens up to each eye. I was quite far away from the castle at this point. Farther than I had ever been on my own.

I stumbled along in this fashion, past the farmers watering the fields where summer crops such as oats and barley are ripe for the picking. Somebody was approaching me, but I could not tell who it was. I hoped it wasn't one of the castle guards that Mum sent out to find me. I was relieved when the person turned out to be a peasant boy of eleven or twelve. He was wearing a thin brown tunic and sandals. A satchel of freshly picked grapes hung across his chest, and a light film of perspiration shone on his forehead.

"Is everything all right, sire?" the boy asked in a soft voice. He then bent over in an awkward bow. "I have never seen you this far from the castle gates."

I was startled at first, and didn't answer right away. One of the strange things about being in my position is that everyone knows me, but I do not know them.

He pointed at my hands. "Are those your specs? Are they broken, then?"

I nodded, feeling the heat rise to my cheeks. I knew I didn't look very princely with my broken glasses and dusty clothes.

"My papa can fix them, if you wish, sire," the boy said. "He can fix anything." He looked like he wanted to say more about his father, but then simply asked, "Do you want to come to my house, then? It is just down the path in the village."

I hesitated. The boy sounded so sincere, and I admit I was curious to see his home. Plus, I might otherwise stumble around until nighttime — or until Mum realized I was missing and sent out the castle guards.

"Thank you, yes," I said. "That would be very kind."

The boy bowed again, awkwardly.

"Truly, that is not necessary," I told him as we started walking down the dirt road alongside the forest. With light pressure on my arm, he gently guided me along. As we headed into the village, I asked, "What do they call you?"

"My name is Benjamin, sire."

I grinned at him. "Just like mine!"

He looked confused. "Um, yes, sire, I am named after

you. Every boy in the kingdom born the three years following your birth is named Benjamin."

I stopped dead in my tracks. "Surely you jest?"

"N . . . no, sire. Did you not know?"

"I did not. No one ever told me." Father and I would be
having some words upon my return to the castle. "Dare I
ask how many Benjamins there are?" I held my breath.

The other Benjamin said, "I would wager, oh, about fifty
or so in this village alone."

I nearly fainted! Fifty boys named after me? The responsibility! If my place in history is a poor one, they will be
shamed, too.

"Uh, are you all right, Prince Benjamin? You have gone
white."

A few deep breaths later, I nodded. We kept walking.
Children ran everywhere, laughing and dodging their mothers. I tried to ignore the odors wafting out of the fishmonger's
shop. The butchery was not much better. The other Benjamin
didn't seem to notice. Two men were arguing in front of the
blacksmith shop but immediately stopped when we passed
by. "G'day, Prince," one of the men said hesitantly. He probably bowed, but in my current state of blindness, he was too
far away for me to tell for sure. I can only imagine what he
thought was going on, me being led by the arm through the
streets of the village.

We turned a corner and Other Benjamin (that is what I have decided to call him) led me into a very small, round house that seemed to be made only of earth and straw and rock. A hole in the middle of the thatched roof let out the smoke from the fire his mother was tending. I lifted a lens to my eye and saw that his father and younger brother were eating a small meal at the table. They scrambled to their feet when they noticed us. His father brushed off his shirt and bowed. He was round-faced and kind-looking. The young boy just stared at me, mouth hanging open.

"Father, I told Prince Benjamin that you would be able to help him. He has broken his specs."

Unable to think of anything else to do to end the awkwardness, I held the two pieces up so he could see them.

"I will try," he said with what I thought was a wink. While we waited, Other Benjamin's mother fed me tea and some sort of raisin-nut cake that was delicious. The house was tiny, but it was cozy.

Ten minutes later, my glasses had been miraculously put back together with thin thread and a putty of some kind that came out of a small jar. I could not even tell where they had been broken.

I slipped them onto my face. They fit better than ever before. "You are a master at what you do," I said sincerely.

"A master?" the younger brother squeaked. "At cleaning dung heaps?"

Everyone's face reddened, including mine. Other Benjamin's mother said, "Hush, child!"

Other Benjamin's father cleared his throat, stood a little straighter, and said, "Being a spectacle maker is an uncertain line of work. You never know how many folks will need specs, but everyone needs their dung heap cleaned. It's steady business."

I did not know what to say. I never had to think about what profession would be best for raising a family. I had never thought of so many things. I held out my hand and, in my most princely voice, managed to thank him again for a job well done. He had a firm and hearty shake. Then I turned to my namesake. "Thank you, too, Other Benjamin. You were very kind to help me in this way."

Other Benjamin blushed and gave me another clumsy bow.

As I walked back through the village, I took note of all the hardworking folk. The blacksmith steadily banging his iron ore, the coopers bending rims of metal to make their barrels, the farmers lugging buckets of wheat to be ground by the miller. I wondered how many *other* Other Benjamins I was passing.

I have a newfound respect for the villagers who will clean dung heaps instead of following their dream because it is best for their family. They deserve a strong leader to look up to. I better start acting like one. I will enlist Andrew to tell me how. His training for knighthood includes learning all about how nobility is supposed to behave. He'll steer me rightly, I am sure.

CHAPTER EIGHT

～ Rapunzel ～

7th of Augustus

It occurs to me that I have not had to, shall we say, rid my body of excess food or drink since my arrival. I suspect the witch has somehow bewitched my meals so I will not have to relieve myself. This is a good thing, because there is no chamber pot in my room, and I am certainly NOT relieving myself out the window!

CHAPTER NINE

← Prince Benjamin →
7th of Augustus

Andrew and I munch on late-night plum cakes while the night cook sleeps off his six mugs of ale on a stool in the corner of the kitchen. It always amazes me that he doesn't fall off. Even the creaking of our old wooden chairs does not stir him. It took me many years to realize that once the furniture in the castle gets too worn or broken, it is moved into the servants' quarters. These old chairs are so well worn that our rear ends fit perfectly into the indentations created by decades of rear ends. The ones in the Great Hall offer little comfort but can always be relied on to provide a new splinter. I do not see how that is preferable.

"Fifty?" Andrew says, shaking his head in amazement. "Fifty little Benjamins running around the village? That is truly something, my friend."

"They are not so little," I tell him. "Some are only a year younger than us. It was quite a shock, I assure you."

Andrew takes another bite and, with his mouth full, says, "No doubt, friend, no doubt."

It is my turn to shake my head at him. "You shall surely fail your test to become a squire one month hence if you keep talking with your mouth full. You recall the famous saying, 'A page is made a squire only if found worthy of being a knight.'"

"I know, I know," he says, brushing the crumbs from his lap onto the floor. "I've heard that one since I was in the cradle. Trust me, friend. I will not eat stolen plum cakes while showing off my prowess with a sword."

"See that you don't," I say with a smile. I munch my cake quietly, staring out the window into the inky darkness of the castle grounds. "You are so lucky, Andrew," I tell him, not for the first time. "Everyone looks up to a knight. Those fifty Benjamins will certainly admire you for your power and grace."

"They will look up to a king, too," Andrew replies. "As they do a prince."

I shake my head. "They may look at a prince or a king with respect or allegiance, but not with admiration. It is different." I sigh deeply. "I wish there were some way to prove my worthiness. I would dearly like to help the poor spectacle-maker-turned-dung-heap-cleaner. But he is surely too proud to accept charity from me. I would not want to insult him. I must figure out a way for him to get enough money on his own, so that he can become who he has always dreamed of becoming. But how? Ask the castle stonemasons to build more dung chutes around the kingdom so he will have more to clean?"

Andrew wrinkles his nose. "I'm sure there is a better solution than that." He shoots a quick look over at the cook. Still snoring away. He leans forward in his chair and whispers, "You could always search out the secret cave in the Great Forest where the bandits hid their treasure before they were captured. Then you could lead the boy you call Other Benjamin to it while pretending you had not been there before. That way he would rightfully have claim to half of the treasure and it would not be charity."

"What cave? What bandits? What treasure? Have you drunk too much ale yourself?"

Andrew laughs. "You know nothing of the abandoned bandit cave in the woods? I have known of the bandit cave since before I could walk."

My cheeks redden. "Just another example of how my parents keep me in the dark about the truly interesting things in life."

I must look as depressed as I feel, because Andrew pushes the last plum cake toward me and says, "I am sorry, Prince. I didn't mean to make fun. The cave is a crazy idea, anyway."

I shake my head. "No, it's a very good idea. Better than

more dung chutes, that is for certain. Now, I may not know much about the ways of the world, but I do know that a cave full of treasure does not stay full of treasure for long. Would not someone have cleaned it out by now?"

"Ah," replies Andrew, leaning back in his chair, "that is the rub. You see, there is a catch."

"A catch?"

He nods. "A big hairy troll guards the entrance of the cave. No one will dare approach it, not even the knights."

"A troll?" I echo in disbelief. "You are pulling my leg."

"I assure you I am not," Andrew replies. "Your legs are quite long enough as they are."

See, this is why I need a friend like Andrew. No one else would say a thing like that to the prince of the castle. When Andrew first came to live here, six years ago, we were exactly the same height. In the years since, my legs have sprouted a life of their own and I have shot up nearly a foot! "Just so I am clear — you are telling me that somewhere out in the forest, a big hairy troll stands guard over a secret cave full of abandoned bandit treasure. Is that correct?"

"Correct," Andrew replies with a wide grin. His teeth glow white by the dusky light of the oil lamp. I must remember to ask him sometime how he gets them so clean.

I continue. "And this troll is so fearsome that even the bravest knights in the kingdom refuse to face him."

"Correct again."

"And although even the bravest knights quiver in the presence of this troll, I, Prince Benjamin, who has never even been allowed inside the forest, am supposed to conquer the troll and claim the treasure?"

"Yes!" says Andrew enthusiastically. "You will certainly be a hero then. Admired near and far. Traveling minstrels will sing songs of your greatness, yessir!"

"Songs of your greatness, yessir!" the cook mumbles in his sleep. His eyelids flutter but remain closed.

"*Shh*, c'mon," I whisper to Andrew. We try not to scrape the floor too loudly when we push back the chairs. He leads the way with the lamp and we ascend the narrow stairs to the second floor where our bedchambers are located. When we reach my doorway, I tell him, "I think it will be a while before I fight any trolls. But I thank you for your confidence in me."

"I shall not give up," he says, before turning toward his own quarters around the corner. "They will sing of you yet!" As he disappears into the darkness, he whistles a little tune that I recognize as the ballad the jester was singing the night Elkin and I were caught behind the couch. I surely doubt there will ever be songs of Prince Benjamin rescuing any damsels in distress or fighting off big hairy trolls. The bravest act I have thus far committed was to jump in the moat to rescue Annabelle, who had leaned in too far to pet a duck. In my hurry to get her into the waiting arms of our hysterical Mum, I scraped both of my legs on the moat wall. Instead of applying bandages, the royal doctor insisted on placing leeches on my thighs. I cannot understand why he thought it best to have more blood sucked from me whilst I was still bleeding.

It took a fortnight before the smell of the moat was off me.

Father did make a special toast in my honor at supper that night, and I got an extra portion of rutabaga pie. Still, it was nothing to write a song about.

CHAPTER TEN

～ Rapunzel ～

8th of Augustus

I wake up still full from supper, which is a good thing because, for the first time, no breakfast plate awaits me. As much as it pains me to admit it, last night's meal was delicious down to the last pea. Better than Mother makes, for sure, and Mother has a fresh garden and a magical herb to work with. I do not see any garden from my window here, only treetops and birds. Where did the vegetables come from, then? And the pig! Surely no pigs are running wild in the forest.

Sir Kitty slept in the crook of my arm all night, and I was grateful for her warmth. Whenever I woke up in the night — which was often — I heard the rhythmic breathing again . . . but it wasn't coming from her. Each time I heard it, I sat straight up, frantically lit a candle, and searched the room. Nobody was ever there. I feel pretty stupid now because I have used up all my candles. I had five and managed to use them up in three nights. I am not looking forward to the coming sunset, when I will be plunged into darkness with only the faint light of the moon to see by. And what if it is a cloudy night and I hear the breathing again and the moon sheds no light? I shiver at the thought of it.

But night seems far off now. The whole day stretches ahead of me like a big empty void. If I were at home, WHERE I SHOULD BE, I would be helping Mother in the kitchen, practicing my harmonica, mending my clothes, reading stories about princes and princesses and damsels in distress, playing jacks with the neighborhood children, tending the garden with Father, or perhaps getting a jump on next year's lessons. Okay, I probably wouldn't be doing the last one. But I cannot do *any* of those things here.

It hits me that *I* am one of those damsels in distress. What damsel could be in more distress than I? I rack my brain to think of what someone would do in one of those stories. I'll tell you what she WOULDN'T do. She wouldn't just sit here wondering what to do. She would be thinking of a way to escape! I have already tried pushing on the stone walls and none of the stones budge.

As far as I can tell, the only way in or out is through that window. That'll have to be it, then. I shall climb out the window and make my way down the side of the tower. As Father used to say, the simplest solution is often the best.

If I think about it too long, I shall chicken out. So I put on my shoes, slip Sir Kitty into the deep pocket of my dress, and prepare for my descent. Before I climb up onto the ledge, I wrap my braid around the back of my head and use every one of my pins to secure it. I know it's impossible, but it seems like my hair has grown another FOOT since yesterday. It actually drags on the FLOOR when I walk!

Once the braid is as out of the way as it's ever going to be, I back up to the window and hoist myself up a few inches until I am sitting on the ledge. Then I swivel around and let my feet dangle outside. Both hands grip the inside walls on either side of the window. I make the mistake of glancing down and wind up gripping the walls even harder.

DO NOT LOOK DOWN.

I sit still for a few minutes, gathering my strength. It is actually quite pleasant to be outdoors again, after a fashion. I take a deep breath, filling my lungs with the fresh air. Then I move my hands to the ledge on either side of me and, in one fell swoop, manage to flip my body around so I am now facing the tower and dangling from the ledge by my hands. I am careful to stay far enough away from the wall so Sir Kitty doesn't get squashed. My feet search frantically for stones to perch on, but they just keep slipping. How could there be no footholds? This tower must be ancient; surely the weather has worn down the smooth edges.

While I am contemplating what to do next, my left shoe simply FALLS RIGHT OFF MY FOOT. I watch in horror as it bumps the side of the tower a few times and lands in the bushes with a soft *woomph*. Did the witch hear that? Is she anywhere around? I don't dare move. Or breathe. Okay, I have to move. And breathe. My hands are about to give out. Maybe losing the shoe wasn't such a bad thing. I'd probably have better luck getting a toehold with an actual toe. I slide my bare foot against the wall, feeling for cracks. But it is for naught. Perhaps the simplest idea only appears to be the best. Using the last of my strength, I heave myself up and back through the window. I place Sir Kitty on the "bed" and she looks at me accusingly and starts washing again. That cat is very clean.

So much for my great escape. At least I tried. If I can't leave on my own, perhaps I can get someone's attention. A hunter, or a knight, or a traveling merchant. I'd even settle for a wayward bandit. But how? I don't dare scream — the witch would probably hear it before any rescuer did — and even if I still had candles left, they wouldn't give off enough smoke to make smoke signals. Nor would my matches. I look around the small room for ideas and find myself turning in circles. So I keep turning. Faster and faster I whirl, my dress swirling around my legs, my head spinning. I do not stop twirling until I am so dizzy that I fall into a heap on the rug.

Well, that was mildly entertaining. Not, you know, HUGELY, but somewhat. I wipe the sweat from my brow with my forearm and lie there panting. Perhaps spinning isn't a very productive use of my time, but it took my mind off my situation by scrambling my brains for a few seconds. I shall have to try it again. I stand up and am about to begin again when an unfamiliar odor wafts by. It smells like . . . rotten eggs?? I had no breakfast, and the witch did not leave eggs last night, I am sure of it. I quickly get to my feet and search the room. No eggs anywhere, but I still smell them. Odd. Gradually it dawns on me that the smell is coming from me! From my ARMPITS!

Mother always laid out my clothes each morn. Without her to do that, it hadn't occurred to me to change out of my birthday dress. How pathetic am I! I need my mother to tell me when to change my clothes? For the first time, it truly sinks in that I am on my own here. Possibly forever. Sir Kitty has moved from the table to the window ledge. I hope she isn't planning on trying that means of escape. Has she learned nothing from my failure? I pick her up and hug her close to my chest.

I am sure no one will blame me if a few teardrops land on her head.

While she purrs in my arms, I watch out the window as the birds swoop above the trees, darting in and out as though playing hide-and-seek with each other. They are so free and don't even realize it. I didn't realize how free *I* was until this happened to me. Perhaps no one does until it is taken away. After a few minutes of feeling sorry for myself, I take a deep breath, put the cat back on top of the little table, and head over to my trunk. I am NOT going to let this evil witch break me. She may be able to rob me of my family and my childhood, but she CANNOT make me smell!

I pull out the five dresses I brought with me and choose my favorite. Mother bought me this dress for my first day of school last year. It was the first dress she ever purchased from a merchant at the market rather than sewing herself. It has blue ruffles on the collar and also at the ends of the short sleeves. The white skirt falls in pleats to just above my knees. I pull my birthday dress over my head and go to stuff it back in the trunk when I realize that it will just make everything else smell. The yellow stripes are now gray with the dust and dirt of the tower. But I have nothing to wash it with.

I slip on the new dress, which smells nice and fresh like the lavender that Mother mixes with sheep's fat and ashes to make her special soaps. Sometimes Father will leave his shirts outside in the wind to air them out; perhaps that would work for me, too. On the left side of the window are some iron hinges that must once have held a swinging windowpane. It takes me a few tries, but I finally manage to secure the dress to one of the hinges by wrapping the sash tightly around it. The rest of the dress is now hanging out the window, blowing in the breeze. The forest smells of pine and cedar, and I am pleased with my innovative solution. I am sure by tomorrow morning the dress will smell like new.

I hear a little *plop* behind me and figure Sir Kitty has jumped off the table to the floor. But when I turn around, I see she is still lying on the table, cleaning her foot with her tongue. So what was the plop? I glance around and catch sight of an oval-shaped object sitting in the middle of the rug. I bend over it. It is an oil lamp made of copper and glass! And it is filled with oil! I bet there is enough oil in there to last for weeks. Is it possible that the witch is kinder than I thought? Why else would she leave this for me? I put it away, deciding to take it out only at night. For the first time since my arrival, I feel a tiny surge of hope, quickly followed by gratitude that she hadn't arrived just a little bit earlier. She would have found me hanging from the window ledge!

CHAPTER ELEVEN

✦ Prince Benjamin ✦

8th of Augustus

Elkin is back! I cannot believe it! His parents have determined he would get better training at becoming a "responsible adult worthy of marrying a princess" at our castle than their own. Mum says this is because there is no discipline at Elkin's home and he was never taught things like:

1. Boys his age do not pass gas at the table just to get a laugh out of the younger children present (meaning Annabelle and me). For the record, I do not actually laugh when Elkin passes gas; I gag and it comes out as a laugh. Annabelle, I cannot vouch for.
2. Good grooming is important. It is not a joke to cut off all of one's hair with the gardener's shears before the eleventh birthday of your cousin (me again), thereby ruining the family portrait that the castle artisan had been painting all day.
3. Do not disobey other people's fathers (especially when

they are the king) and lure younger cousins (again, me) into trouble by hiding behind couches.

The list goes on. I can see Mum's point. Elkin truly is rough around the edges. Mum has given me the choice to attend Elkin's training classes. Or, I should say, she has made it appear that she is giving me the choice, when we all know full well that no such choice exists. What she doesn't know is that I would have asked to participate even if I had not been invited. Now that I have learned of the fifty (50!!) other Benjamins looking up to me, I realize that I, too, would benefit from some studies in Future Kingness. Our lessons begin tomorrow. I have practiced holding out my hand so that Andrew can kiss my (imaginary) ring, but he did not appreciate the gesture and I think he is a bit miffed at me.

CHAPTER TWELVE

～♡ Rapunzel ♡～

8th of Augustus

I have thought of a way to escape! It is so obvious. All I have to do is pretend to be asleep when the witch comes with my next meal and watch how she is getting in and out. That's even simpler than my old plan! Since I have had no food yet today, and she left none when she brought the oil lamp, I expect her arrival before nightfall. I am lying on my "bed" with my eyes mostly — but not totally — closed. Time is passing ridiculously slowly. My belly is grumbling. WHERE IS SHE?

WHY IS MY HAIR GROWING SO FAST? What IS she putting in my food?? If I think too much about it, I shall surely go mad.

What is that smell? Herrings? Warm bread? Surely I must be imagining it, because I did not close my eyes so there is no way the witch got by me. Then I hear a slurping sound. I quickly sit up to find Sir Kitty sipping from a bowl of goat's milk on a tray next to BOILED HERRINGS AND STEAMING BLACK BREAD! I also notice that I have to squint to see the food because the sun has nearly set! I cannot BELIEVE I fell asleep! I am the worst spy ever!

I hurry to the table and join Sir Kitty in our evening meal. How could the witch be so cruel to me when I see her and then be kind enough to leave a bowl of milk for the cat? There is more here than meets the eye. I am going to figure it out.

After all, what else have I got to do?

NEXT MORNING, 9TH OF AUGUSTUS

I quickly fall asleep again, and wake to find the sunlight streaming in the window and the witch STANDING OVER MY BED waving my birthday dress in one hand and my fallen shoe in the other. Her face is purple with rage. This can't be good. I scramble to my feet and instinctively back away. I guess this isn't the best time to thank her for the lamp and the bowl of milk. She holds up the items and waves them at me.

"Would you care to offer an explanation for why I found these in the bushes?" she asks through gritted teeth.

I hurry to explain that the dress must have slipped from the window hinge as it was airing out. The shoe is harder to explain. "Er, I thought I saw a dragon last night and I threw my shoe at it?" Okay, so I'm not the world's best liar.

She stares into my eyes with her beady black ones, and I force myself not to look away. Father always says, if you're going to lie, you have to commit to the lie.

"Silly girl," she hisses. "There are no dragons anymore."

"I did not think there were witches, either," I mutter under my breath.

"Do I need to board that window up?"

"Please, no!" I beg, horrified at the thought of losing my one connection to the outside world. "It won't happen again, I promise."

"See that it does not," she says, throwing my dress and shoe on top of my trunk. "I do not give second warnings. Now stand by the window and hold your cheeky tongue."

As I hurry to the window, I feel the weight of something in my pocket. My mirror! I must have stuck it in there last night. My mind races. Keeping my back slightly hunched, I slip my hand into my dress pocket and slowly lift out the mirror and hold it facing me at waist level. Then I tilt it so that I can look down at it and see behind me. If it is possible for a heart to explode by beating fast, surely mine would right now.

It is working! I can see the "bed" and the table. But I do not see the witch. My heart sinks. Then I catch sight of something in the corner of the mirror and tilt it up a smidge more. I can just make out what looks like a rope being pulled into the ceiling! I tilt the mirror even more and see the rope disappear and a trapdoor soundlessly being pulled closed. THERE IS A TRAPDOOR IN THE CEILING! I can barely contain myself. I want to sing. To do a jig. To laugh and laugh. I have found my way out!

CHAPTER THIRTEEN

← Prince Benjamin →

9th of Augustus

Our lessons have begun, and Father is teaching. He claps his hands once, and a page appears at his side carrying two pillows with gold crowns on them. Father places the first crown on my head, and the other on Elkin's.

"We shall practice your regal bearing," he says, standing back and sizing us up.

Elkin and I stare at each other's head. I haven't worn a crown since I tried on one of Father's when I was six, only to have it fall around my neck and land on my shoulders. It would have been funny if the tips of the crown hadn't punctured my neck in four places. But this crown stays squarely atop my head. I really AM growing up! Or perhaps just my head is. Either way, I am pleased.

"Back straight," Father commands in that commanding voice of his. "Head forward, chin raised slightly. Arms at your sides."

I hear *crickity-crack-pop* as I straighten my back. Why

didn't anyone tell me I had such poor posture? I sound like an old man!

"Now, a king must always be gracious and courteous. When somebody bows to you, or gives you a gift, or pays their taxes on time, you will want to acknowledge them. A king does not bow, but tilts his head and adds a little bob, like this." Father tips his head forward and to the side, then adds a small bob, like he is nodding once at the person, but sideways. Elkin and I imitate him. Elkin is better at it. With my long neck, I look not unlike a chicken.

"Gobble, gobble, gobble," Elkin whispers, but not loud enough for Father to hear.

Father instructs me not to bob quite so *large,* and to my further humiliation, I try too hard and strain a muscle in my neck. The muscle has completely seized up and I cannot turn my head to the left. Father sends for Mum, who wants to send for the doctor. I convince her to call for the royal masseuse instead. The doctor is way too quick with those leeches.

CHAPTER FOURTEEN

~⊃ Rapunzel ⊂~

9th of Augustus, later

It seems I have NOT found my way out. Just because I know the trapdoor exists, what made me think I could reach it? The ceiling is at least five times taller than I. Jumping up got me nowhere. Standing on the table did not help much, either. Standing on the chair on top of the table brought me about halfway, but that was all.

All the activity has made my new dress smell and I have to change it. At this rate, I shall run out of clothes before the end of the week! I dare not hang this one out the window, and even after its night outside, my birthday dress still smells like Father's old socks. It is a good thing I am too young to marry, for no one wants to marry a smelly girl. Or one locked in a tower, for that matter.

To take my mind off the tantalizing yet out-of-reach trapdoor, I entertain myself (and I use that term loosely) by using the sooty ends of my old matchsticks to trace the pattern of the sun as it travels the length of my floor. Sir Kitty is down here with me, pouncing on the line as soon as I draw it. All day I am on my knees marking the shadow as it grows larger until finally the whole room is in shade. In my own special way, I am connecting with nature. Father would be proud. He always told me the reason he loves tending the garden is because he never feels closer to the source of life than while helping something grow. (Of course, now I know that what he was helping grow has brought my downfall!) After I am done with the floor, I move on to the wall. With my last two used matchsticks, I draw the outline of the cottage where, until this week, I had rested my head every night of my life. I draw the window that looks into Mother's sewing room and add a wisp of smoke out the chimney. Fittingly enough, the ash on my last matchstick runs out as I am about to draw the garden where my abduction took place.

I have decided to keep the mirror with me at all times so I can learn more about the door and rope system. With the mirror titled backward in my hand, I bide my time at the window. It is dusk now, and the forest has quieted. Even the ever-present blackbirds have gone to their nests for the night. Suddenly I realize there is a reflection in my mirror, and it is moving quickly! I watch, fascinated, as the witch shinnies down the rope, much faster than I ever imagined she could move. She reaches the ground and bends over to place a tray of food on the rug. That's when I notice it:

THIS IS NOT THE WITCH!!!

I almost drop the mirror but manage to tighten my grasp just in time. Whoever this is, he is much smaller than the witch, with a bald head and pale green skin. GREEN SKIN! I am terrified to move a muscle, so I wait until the creature climbs back up the rope. He pulls it back up in the blink of an eye and shuts the door. All of this was in complete silence. My ragged breathing is the only thing I heard the whole time.

I race over to the center of the room and stare up at the ceiling. My legs are shaking, so I sit down on the rug before I fall over. What WAS that? I finally collect my wits enough to look at the food. Meat pie, two hard-boiled eggs, one jellied pastry, a mug of cider, and another bowl of milk. This is my best meal yet! As I reach hungrily for the plate, my eyes land on a small white bag tied with a drawstring. I lift it up and it gives off a sweet scent. I undo the drawstring and peek inside. It is a ball of soap! Instead of lavender, though, it is scented with pine, just like the breeze outside.

Suddenly it all makes sense. A fog clears like a veil being lifted and I can finally see. This *creature* has been bringing me the gifts. The bowls of milk, the oil lamp, and now the soap. The witch knows nothing about it! How can I let this creature know how much I appreciate his kindness? I hurry over to my trunk and pull out a piece of vellum, my quill, and the ink. In my neatest penmanship, I write:

Dear Little Green Creature,
Thank you well and truly for the milk and the
lamp and the soap. I am deeply in your debt. I
am certain this was a risk for you, and I am
grateful. Please talk with me next time instead of
leaving so hurriedly. I am desperate for company
and should like to thank you in person.
With much sincerity,
Rapunzel, tower prisoner

I fold the note in half and slip it under the plate. Then I dig into my meal with both hands. No need for manners here.

CHAPTER FIFTEEN

← Prince Benjamin →

10th of Augustus

I have almost fully recovered from yesterday's lessons in regal bearing. I have had a neck rub from the royal masseuse, and the local apothecary ground some herbs into a salve that I rub on every hour. Even so, Mum is insisting that I stay in bed with warm linens wrapped around my neck. I'm sure Elkin would be teasing me relentlessly had Father not recruited him for more lessons. So now he is off with MY father learning all about castle politics, giving alms to the poor, and who KNOWS what else. It is simply not fair.

Andrew peeks his head into my room and asks, "How is the patient?"

I grunt in reply. He enters, holding a rolled-up parchment in one hand and an old book in the other. He places the book on the night table and waves the parchment in his hand.

"What's that?" I ask, pushing myself up into a sitting position.

"This, sire," he says dramatically, "is your future!" With

a flick of his wrist, he unfurls the yellowed sheet and spreads it out on the foot of my bed.

I lean closer. "It looks like a map of the Great Forest."

"It IS a map of the Great Forest!" he exclaims. "And with it you shall find the bandits' cave, marked by this X!" He thrusts his finger down onto a far corner of the map.

I groan and lie back down again. "You're still thinking about that crazy idea? Have you forgotten about the legendary troll that makes grown knights tremble?"

"I knew you'd say that," he said, reaching for the book on the night table. "So I came prepared with this."

"Why am I afraid to look?"

He hands me the book and I see it is even older than I had first thought. The tooled leather that covers the oak covers is ripped in many places, and the stitching is falling apart as well. Even with my glasses on, I have to squint to read the faded gold-leaf title. *Trolls: Inside and Out — A User's Manual.* I should have guessed.

"No, thank you." I hand the book back to him. "I don't want to know about the insides of a troll."

He leaves me holding it. "Just give it a quick read. It tells you their weaknesses. You could learn enough to vanquish it and save the day for all the other Benjamins out there."

"They really *could* use the money," I murmur, resting my

palm on the book. "And I *would* like to prove I am worthy of being named after."

"That is the spirit!" Andrew says, clapping his hands together. "Now, how are we going to get you into the forest? To discourage bandits, your father has decreed that only the royal hunters are allowed entrance."

We are pondering this question when Elkin strolls in, munching on a crab apple. He eyes the map curiously, and Andrew snatches it off my bed and hastily rolls it back up.

"Can I help you, Elkin?" I ask sweetly. No use being antagonistic. Bad for the soul.

Elkin glances suspiciously at Andrew and the rolled-up parchment, but says only, "Your father wanted me to alert you that we shall be taken on our first hunt six days hence."

Andrew and I exchange a look and my heart leaps a little.

"IF you are better, of course," Elkin adds.

"He will be," Andrew answers before I have a chance.

CHAPTER SIXTEEN

∽ Rapunzel ∽

10th of Augustus

When I woke up today, the supper tray with my hidden note was gone. I hope my new friend found it. I hope I did not insult him by addressing the letter to "Little Green Creature." If I had known his rightful name, I certainly would have used it. What if the witch found the note instead? I would lose the only ally I have. I shudder to think of what would happen to the little guy if he got caught giving me gifts. Have I put him in danger? Was I thinking only of my own needs?

Meanwhile, my hair keeps getting longer and longer.

CHAPTER SEVENTEEN

⇠ Prince Benjamin ⇢

11ᵗʰ of Augustus

The hunt is in a few days and I am off to meet Andrew in the courtyard to discuss the plan. I have just finished reading the book on trolls from cover to cover and am ready for whatever I might find at the cave. Or at least I am telling myself that I am ready, in the hopes that I may come to believe it. I learned only two things from the book:

1. Trolls are huge, scary, hairy, and hungry, which I pretty well knew already. They will eat anything, from the smallest berry to the largest horse. To illustrate its point, the book thoughtfully included artists' renderings of the trolls eating exactly that. I shall have nightmares for weeks.

2. Trolls are highly, even deathly, allergic to tomatoes. Something in the flesh of the tomato is poisonous to their system. They don't even need to eat it. Merely getting it on their skin will do the damage. I plan on

stuffing as many tomatoes as I can in my saddlebags. They will be my main mode of defense.

Andrew has the map spread out on the stone bench when I arrive, and is drawing on it with the edge of a piece of coal. "This is where the hunting party will begin," he says, marking a small X at one entrance to the forest. "Most of the group will head into the heart of the forest near the head of the stream. That is where they will find the greatest number of animals." He draws a path leading away from the stream. "But once the party has separated, you will quietly ride off to the west, where the cave should be."

My already low amount of confidence is dwindling. "Are you sure I'll be all right riding through the forest on my own?" I ask. "What if the cave-guarding troll isn't the worst creature there?"

"What's worse than a troll? A goblin? A witch? No one has reported either of those in years. The tomatoes will take care of the troll, and there shall be nothing keeping you from the treasure and the chronicles of history."

"I hope you are correct, Andrew," I say, rolling up the map and sticking it in my leather satchel. "For otherwise it will fall to you to explain why I have not returned with the rest of the hunting party. I'm sure Mum won't take it out on you too badly."

For the first time this morning, Andrew's grin slips and he grimaces, as he says, "I think I'd rather face the troll."

CHAPTER EIGHTEEN

∼ Rapunzel ∼

11ᵗʰ of Augustus

I am beginning to suspect that the witch somehow makes me fall asleep even when I am not tired. One minute it is early afternoon and I am storing my soap safely in my trunk, and the next I am curled up on the "bed," the sun has reached three quarters of the way across the tower floor, and a tray of food is getting cold on the rug. I hurry over and search under every plate and bowl for a response to my note. The extra bowl of milk is here, along with a small plate of sardines that I figure is also for Sir Kitty — and even if it isn't, she has already licked each one, so she will get no argument from me. No reply to my note, though. Well, it was worth a shot. At least the little guy wasn't caught by the witch, and that is the most important thing.

With a sigh, I pick up my wooden spoon and am about to thrust it into the thick vegetable stew when I notice seven peas resting on top. Two next to each other, another centered below them, and four others forming a U-shaped curve underneath the rest. Little Green Creature has left me a happy face! I smile down into the stew, then pick out the peas and pop them in my mouth one by one.

After I lick the bowl clean, I head over to the window. I know the creature will not come again tonight, so I do not bother with the mirror. The sun shall set soon, but for now the forest is still aglow. I used to think that there were only two colors in the forest, the grayish-brown bark of the trees, and the green of the leaves. My time in the tower has taught me otherwise. The greens are not only one color. There is a deep, almost blackish green of the lower leaves; a green the shade of a ripe lime; a green that looks yellow when the sun lights it. Besides the array of greens, every color of the rainbow lives here. The bushes that ring the tower base are home to purple and red berries, which look round and succulent although I can only stare down longingly at them. Father has told me never to eat strange berries, but surely he did not know of these, nor of the plump oranges that grow in a grove west of my window. Sometimes they still glow after the sun has set as though lit from a candle within. It used to be a rare treat when Mother brought oranges home from the weekend market, but here they are for the picking. (Not by me, of course, but someone who is NOT trapped in a tower by an evil witch could surely pick them with no problem.)

I wait until I can see the first star before lighting my lamp.

The flickering wick casts interesting shadows on the ceiling. If I peer closely, I can see the lines where the trapdoor opens better than I can during the sunlit day. Will I never discover what is above there? A feeling of resolve comes over me. I am NOT going to be defeated so easily. I walk over to the wall and trace my finger over the lines of the cottage I drew there, careful not to smear the ash as I go. I shall get back there one day for certain. For a girl who never spent a day on her own before, I have gained a strength I never would have guessed I owned.

"Are you up there?" I call out as loud as I dare.

No response.

I try again, a little louder. "Little green guy? Sir?" My voice reverberates off the walls and sounds unfamiliar to my ears.

Still no response. I rummage through the trunk to find things to throw up at the ceiling. Aiming for the center of the trapdoor, I hurl my comb, but it spins wildly and hits nowhere near the door. I try with the tin of ointment, which not only does not reach the ceiling but falls down with surprising force and smacks me on the knee. Now I have to use the ointment to avoid a bruise! It smells of rampion, its main ingredient, and I try not to breathe in the fresh smell of my enemy.

I have better luck with my boots, in that they at least hit the upper parts of the walls before plummeting. By this time, I have learned to stand back so I do not fall victim to their plunge. While I am putting everything back in the trunk, Sir Kitty stretches her paw at me from the straw bed and gets it tangled in my braid. I would tug the braid away, but it would not do much good. My hair is so long now, I'm surprised when there ISN'T a paw tangled in there! As I watch her try to get untangled, a new plan begins to form. I remove her paw and take the belt out of my trunk, the one with the little silver bells that I was wearing on my birthday (now forever known as The Day Of My Kidnapping). I pull out the hairpins that hold my hair to my neck and shake my braid loose. Then I tie the belt around the very end of my hair where the pink (now gray) ribbons have been holding the strands of hair together. For the record, once the braid unfurls, I have to pull, hand over hand, for quite a long time to even REACH the very end of my hair.

I drag the small table to the center of the room and carefully balance myself on top. With all my might, I heave my hair into the air, almost heaving myself off the table at the same time. The end of the braid actually gets pretty good height before falling back down and hitting the floor beneath me, the jingling of the bells slightly muted by the rug. I climb down, gather my hair back up, and try again. If the ghost who haunts this place is watching, I hope she's having a good laugh. I am certain I must look quite ridiculous. On

the sixth attempt, the belt hits its target. The jingling reverberates through the tower. That should do it! If the creature
IS on the other side, he surely would have heard that. I sit
back down on the "bed" to wait. I wait and wait, my neck
cocked back, not taking my eyes off the ceiling. Sir Kitty
falls asleep in my lap. My neck finally gets sore and I lie
down, trying to swallow the disappointment. Perhaps the
smiling peas were just peas.

CHAPTER NINETEEN

← Prince Benjamin →

11ᵗʰ of Augustus

It is tax collection day. Father has instructed Elkin and me to stand at his side while the villagers come to pay their taxes. The royal tax collector sits behind his large oak desk logging the payments in his large, leather-bound journal. Even the quill he uses is large. The royal tax collector himself, however, is not large. Quite the opposite. He is even shorter than Elkin and must sit on top of ledgers from years past in order to reach the desktop. After each villager hands over his bag of coins and has his name recorded in the book, he bows to Father. In turn, Father gives the head-bob in acknowledgement of the payment. Elkin and I have been instructed to follow. With each bob, I feel a sharp pain in my neck where I injured it. After I gasp out loud for the third time, Father relieves me of my neck-bobbing responsibility and instructs me to just smile sincerely instead.

As I am flashing my nicest smile at the latest villager, the man winks at me and says, "How are those specs holding up?"

I quickly recognize him as Other Benjamin's father, as jolly as ever. I glance at Father and Elkin to see if they heard. If the man tells Father about my trip to the village, I may not be allowed to participate in the hunt, and then this nice man, this dutiful taxpayer, will remain a dung heap cleaner forever. Fortunately, Father is busy in conversation with the bailiff, but Elkin is quite attuned. Other Benjamin's father is waiting for a response. "Quite well, thank you, sir." I smile nervously and push my glasses farther up on the bridge of my nose.

"I am glad," he says, and steps down in the line.

As soon as the man is out of earshot, Elkin asks, "What was THAT about?"

I shake my head. "I have no idea. He must have liked my glasses."

"Why would anyone like your glasses?"

"Do stop talking, Elkin."

"Sheesh," Elkin says, head-bobbing at the candlemaker. "Some people are so touchy."

CHAPTER TWENTY

∽ Rapunzel ∾
12ᵗʰ of Augustus

It is still hours away from dawn, yet I cannot sleep. I toss and turn, feeling even more alone than before I knew about the creature. Surely never was there a girl more wretched than I at this moment. I have blown out the small flame. It is easier to feel sorry for oneself in the darkness. As I stare into the gray air around me, I suddenly hear big heaving sobs. Odd. If I am not crying, then who is?

I jump out of "bed" and quickly strike a match to re-light the lamp. As I do, a round green face appears before me, wet from the tears rolling steadily down its cheeks. In my surprise I drop the match, which instantly lights the ends of my straw "bed" on fire! The orange embers are creeping toward the shawl Mother knit for me. Sir Kitty has the sense to run hissing under the table.

In a flash of a second (although it seems like forever, which moments like this tend to do), the green guy stomps out the flames. It is now dark again. Neither of us says a word. Slowly I pick up the matches again, and although my shaking hands make the task more difficult now, I manage to light another one and bring it to the wick. As the room slowly illuminates, I half-expect the creature to be gone again, but I find him standing with his back flattened against the wall. Or at least the bottom half of his back, because the top part is hunched over, his face turned to the ground. Mother would be quite aghast at his posture. Every few seconds, a sniffle or a gentle sob escapes from him. I have never seen a grown man cry and it is a bit unnerving. At least I think he is a grown man. It is hard to tell with green creatures. What does one say in a situation like this?

I clear my throat and say, "Er, are you all right, Mr. Green Creature, sir? I am sorry, but I do not know your proper name."

"St . . . St . . . Steven," he replies in quick breaths.

"Steven?" I repeat. "Your name is *Steven*?"

He takes a deep breath and his breathing steadies. "What were you expecting?" he asks.

I shrug. "Something more exotic, I suppose."

"Exotic like *Rapunzel*?" he asks. "*Rapunzel* is another word for the herb rampion, you know."

I grit my teeth. "Yes, I know. I wish it were not my name."

"I, too, long for a more dashing name. Alas, Steven was my father's name, and his father's before him. It is my son's name too, but . . . but . . ."

He trails off and starts sobbing again. I rush over and put my arm on his bony shoulder. "There, there," I say soothingly. "It will be all right."

He wipes his runny nose with the back of his wrist. There is a lot of hair on his wrist and it neatly absorbs the rather hefty contents of his nose. Perhaps the hair on his arms is so thick to make up for the lack of hair on his head. He looks up at me with watery eyes and asks, "How can you, of all people, say everything will be all right?"

He has a point. I consider my answer. "Well, it's better than saying 'Keep on crying, I'm sure things will just get worse,' right?"

He doesn't answer for a moment, then breaks into a laugh that borders on hysteria. It's a cross between the sound of a creaky door hinge and the noise Father makes when he is choking on a piece of bread. Still, it is better than the sobbing. I must admit that seeing someone even more down in the dumps than I have been has buoyed my spirits somewhat.

"Why don't we sit down on the rug and get to know each other," I suggest. "I have many questions."

Still "laughing," he allows me to steer him to the rug, where we both sit cross-legged. The rope from the open trapdoor swings gently next to us. He pulls himself together, wipes one stray tear from his chin, and says, "I received your note. I am glad my gifts gave you pleasure. You are right that the witch must never know."

"So it WAS you?"

He nods.

"Do you have magic powers, too," I ask, "like the witch?"

He shakes his head again, this time a little sadly. "I can apply only the tricks of the trade — a little sleeping powder here, a dab of hair-growing tonic there. That sort of thing."

I knew my rapid hair growth was not normal! "But why are you doing those things to me?" I ask. Perhaps he is not the friend I thought he was.

"It is not I," he says hurriedly. "I am under orders from the witch — or Mother Gothel, as she insists on being called." After he says her name, he turns to his right and spits once, then repeats the action on his left.

I try not to look at the little puddles of spittle now sinking into my rug. "If you hate her so much, then why are you doing her bidding?"

"I have no choice," he says, his features falling. "I am in debt to her for saving my son's life. We were in the caves — that is where my race lives, underground — and young Stevie suddenly could not breathe. He was gasping for air, clutching his throat. I called out, 'Help! Help! Somebody help!' But no one was around. I carried him above ground, which we are supposed to visit only to gather food when the supply of minerals runs low. Our green color allows us to blend in well with the trees and grass, but we are a private race, you see, and prefer to keep to ourselves. When I reached the air, the forest was still, like it is right after a rain. The only person around was this little old lady. When she saw my problem, she mumbled some sort of incantation, sprinkled some dust, and a bug the size of my hand flew out of Stevie's throat. I mean, this bug, it had fifty legs, antennae the size of my arm, eyes like a —"

I hold up my hand. "I get the picture. It was big."

"SO big! Naturally I asked the woman what I could do to repay her. When someone saves your life, or your child's life, you are indebted to them for life, you know."

I nod. Everyone knows that.

"So the woman told me she needed a cook and a sentry, and did I have any training in either of those fields? As it turned out, I often won awards for my famous dishes, and being the largest of my species for miles around, I frequently had the job of guarding the entry to the caves. I knew now that she was a witch, of course, but assumed she was a good witch. After all, she had saved my son's life! She hired me to do both jobs and I bid a sad good-bye to my family, although in truth I believed I would be able to bring them along once I got settled. I had expected the witch to lead me to her cottage somewhere, but she brought me to this tower instead

~ 83 ~

and led me up a dark, musty staircase. At the top was an attic space where I was to prepare a daily meal. The shelves were stocked full of all the ingredients a cook could ever want. For days I practiced new recipes and wandered in the nearby orange grove. But no one ever ate my food, and there was nothing to guard that I could see. I began to wonder what was going on. Then you showed up." He pauses here to take a deep breath. "And I, still believing the witch was good, believed her when she told me you were being punished for the terrible crime of theft, and I was to feed you one meal a day without being seen. She showed me how the trapdoor worked, and how to oil it nightly so it did not creak. With my natural agility, it was easy to get in and out without being seen."

"Don't forget you had a little help by way of the sleeping powder."

Steven clears his throat. "Well, okay, there was that. But, anyway, it took only a day or two to see that you were not a thief at all. Only a young girl stolen away from her family too soon."

I can't help but lean over and hug him. He may be bony, but I can feel the strength in his arms as well. He had to be strong — and flexible — to get up and down that rope so quickly. I would not like to be the prisoner trying to run past him. Perhaps I won't have to be.

"So you will let me go?"

"Sorry, dear child, but I cannot."

"Yes, you could," I insist. "You could just lift me up on that rope, and I can climb down the staircase from your attic room. You could come WITH me! We would be far from here before she would even notice!"

He shakes his head adamantly. "I am in her service until my debt is paid off. I must fulfill the terms of my job."

"How long is your service, then?"

His brows furrow. He picks a piece of lint off the rug before answering. "As long as I live. Or else young Stevie will die."

I swallow. This witch is surely the most horrid creature in this kingdom or any other. "Then why do you risk her wrath by bringing me gifts?"

His expression lifts a bit at the mention of the gifts. "The witch shows up so rarely, I figure she will not notice. I could not bear to see you so unhappy."

Poor, brave Steven. Risking so much for someone he doesn't even know. I doubt I would be brave enough to do something like that.

Sir Kitty walks up and, as if she understands the situation, rubs her face against Steven's leg and purrs loudly. Steven smiles and picks her up.

"I was so pleased when I saw how much you liked the cat," he says, scratching her belly. "I worried she might make you sneeze."

My eyes widen. "Sir Kitty was a gift from you? I thought she was here before I arrived."

Steven shakes his head. "I found her in the bushes beneath the tower and knew you could use the company."

"But the witch saw her! You could have gotten caught."

"Don't worry," he says, placing Sir Kitty back on the rug. "Your quick thinking saved me. The witch probably believes the kitten got carried in along with the straw for your bed."

"As did I," I tell him, smiling. "You are very sneaky, Master Steven."

"Stop," he says, "you are making me blush."

I cannot help wondering what color blushing cheeks would be on someone who is the color of a lima bean, but I do not want to be rude and peer too closely. "So what do we do? Just stay the witch's prisoners forever?"

"But I am not her prisoner," he reminds me. "Although I can see how it would appear that way. I shall continue to bring you things to make your life here more bearable. And even while you sleep, I am protecting you, although you are unaware."

"But I *was* aware," I tell him, suddenly realizing what I

should have figured out before. "The breathing that lulls me to sleep — that comes from you."

"You can hear my breathing?"

I nod. "I thought it must be a ghost."

He smiles. "My dear wife, Katherine, always tells me I am a heavy breather. Worse than the fluttering of a noble lady's fan, she used to say." His smile slowly fades and he looks sad.

I hope he isn't going to cry again! To cheer him up, I suggest we play a game. I am quite good at chess but, of course, we do not have a set.

"I must decline your kind offer," Steven says, springing up from the rug, looping his arm around the rope, and grasping it with both hands.

Truly, the man (I cannot call him a creature now that we are friends) moves like the acrobat I saw perform once in Market Square.

Steven twists his legs around the end of the rope and says, "It is almost morn, and one never knows when the witch will darken my door."

"When shall I see you again?" I call after him as he slithers up the rope at a speed I would have previously thought quite impossible. By the time I finish my question, he is already closing the trapdoor.

"I am always here when you need me," he calls down as he pulls the door shut. Those hinges certainly *are* greased with magic oil, because they do not make even a whisper. The tower seems smaller, somehow, now that I am alone again. With a sigh, I blow out the wick and climb onto the "bed." I strain my ears until I can hear Steven's rhythmic, steady breathing. I feel myself drifting off to that place where everything is fuzzy but you know you are not yet asleep. Something is nagging at me. It is as though the answer to a riddle is right around the corner of my brain, yet I cannot reach it. I am not even sure what the riddle is, but I know it is vital that I figure it out.

CHAPTER TWENTY-ONE

⤙ Prince Benjamin ⤚
12th of Augustus

Father has called Elkin and me down to the sitting room to go over the rules for the hunt. It is cool for a summer eve, and the three of us are seated in high-back leather chairs in front of the fireplace. Mum and Annabelle are here, too. Mum is busy embroidering gems onto a new dress. (Although she has a large staff to assemble her considerable wardrobe, she says sewing relaxes her. I think Mum and I have more in common in terms of our artistic creativity then she will admit). Annabelle is pretending to play with her collection of tiny wooden dolls, but whenever Mum isn't looking, she throws one of them into the fire. I worry about that child.

Father begins the lecture by talking about the virtues of the longbow versus the crossbow, how one can fire off many more arrows per minute with the longbow, thereby increasing one's chances of successfully reaching one's target. When he moves on to how to keep an animal in your line of sight, I stop listening. I will not be shooting any arrows. Well, unless my tomato assault fails. Even then, I do not think one can vanquish a troll with a bow and arrow. Certainly *I* cannot. While Father speaks, I go over Andrew's map in my head. I figure the better I know the path ahead of time, the swifter I will reach the cave without being missed by the hunting party.

"Benjamin," Father rumbles, "are you listening to me?"

The forest vanishes and I'm back in front of the fire. Elkin is smirking. He'd better be careful or his face will have a permanent smirk and then his soon-to-be wife will not like him (although chances are high that she won't, anyway). "Er, yes, Father," I say, glaring at Elkin.

"Now, due to your recent head-bobbing injury —"

Elkin chuckles and Father does not reprimand him. Nice to stand up for one's own son! His ONLY son and heir, I might add. Although if I fail to vanquish the troll and the troll vanquishes me instead, perhaps Father will decide to adopt Elkin. The horror of it!

"As I was saying, due to your, er, *accident*, you missed practicing with the royal archers yesterday. Elkin did very well and hit all his targets. He is being given a chance to prove he can indeed be a good influence on you, and he will be your guide in the hunt. I want you to stick closely by him. The rest of us will be too busy to watch over you."

Father's words sink in. My plans are ruined! I cannot let this happen. I jump to my feet in protest. "I'll be fine on my own, Father. You know I am a strong rider. Elkin doesn't need me to shadow him. I would just be in his way."

Elkin adds, "Truly he would, uncle. I cannot wait to bag my supper, and what if Benjamin scares the animal off?"

Father shakes his head. "On a young man's first hunt, it is traditional for an older brother or cousin to ride with a younger. In this case, Elkin, you are the elder, so you two shall ride together. I will hear no more about it."

I look pleadingly at Mum. She is engrossed in her sewing and shows no signs of even following the conversation. I slump back into my seat and stare at the fire. I refuse even to glance at Elkin, who I can tell is pouting in that special way of his where he sticks out his lower lip and turns down the corners of his mouth.

"Burn burn burn!" Annabelle squeals gleefully and tosses the last of her dolls into the flames. Mum finally notices what Annabelle has been doing for the past half hour and lunges out of her chair. The dress slips to the floor and the tiny gems fly off her lap and scatter. They appear very bright against the white stone. We all watch in horror as Mum actually reaches her hand into the fire and snatches out the closest doll.

The sleeve of her gown is in flames! She gasps and drops the doll, which unfortunately falls right back into the fire. Annabelle begins to wail and grabs at Mum's skirts. Father reaches Mum first and plunges her arm into the pitcher of water that one of the servants had placed on his desk only moments ago. When she pulls it out, her sleeve is in tatters, but her hand is only slightly pink.

Father wraps his big arms around her and leads her from the room. Annabelle follows, wailing as she goes. In silence, Elkin and I bend down to pick up the gems that have settled into tiny crevices in the floor. We stuff them back into Mum's sewing basket along with the robe. Finally Elkin turns to me and says, "I am not fond of this arrangement any more than you are. I was looking forward to being on my own in the forest."

"So was I." That is an understatement.

"If you prove your skill and come home with supper slung over your back," he says, "I am sure you will no longer need a guide."

I mumble something that is a cross between "not likely" and "good night" and set out to find Andrew. We have a plan to revise.

LATER

"Oh, this is bad," Andrew says, pacing the floor of my bedchamber. He is swinging a twenty-pound anvil with each arm as he walks, building up his strength for his squire test. His muscles are already quite large, but he says the competition is stiff and every muscle counts.

"I suppose the treasure will have to wait till I am allowed to go on the hunt without needing to be watched like a child."

"I fear that Elkin was correct. You will have to prove yourself first. Are you up for bagging a small fox perhaps? Or a hare?"

"Absolutely not! I dislike the very IDEA of hunting."

"Okay, okay, don't bust a gut, we will think of something else."

I sit on my bed, fingering the edges of the map, watching him pace. I have the path to the cave memorized. A fat lot of good that will do me now.

Finally he stops pacing and rests the anvils on the floor. With a deep sigh of resignation, he says, "You'll just have to bring Elkin with you."

"What? Have you drunk too much ale? You know what he's like. He will ruin the whole plan. He will try to keep all the treasure for himself!"

"I am not certain of that," Andrew replies. "Elkin may be unpleasant and rude, but I do not think he is a thief. Further, you are forgetting one important thing."

"And what might that be?"

"The troll! Once Elkin sees the creature, no doubt he will take off at a gallop in the opposite direction, leaving the treasure to you and, later, Other Benjamin."

"But he may not even agree to go with me. Perhaps he'll insist on staying with the hunting party or — worse yet — on telling Father." I wring my hands. "Are there no other options but to involve him?"

Andrew shrugs. "We can wait for the opportunity to present itself again. Of course, Elkin will be leaving in a few weeks, and the only reason you are going on the hunt in the first place is because your father is training him in the ways of being a king."

I jerk my head up. "Truly?"

Andrew's eyebrows rise. "You did not know? Your formal training was not set to begin for another year. So in a way, you owe Elkin for the fact that you are being allowed into the forest at all."

I shake my head sadly. That figures. "Okay. I'll alert him to the plan and hope for the best."

"Hope for the best, but plan for the worst," Andrew says, grasping my shoulder. "That is a knight's motto."

"Great motto," I mumble. "And, ow, that hurt."

"Sorry — don't know my own strength."

I rub my sore shoulder. And I thought the troll would be the worst part of this venture. But no, it's my froglike cousin!

CHAPTER TWENTY-TWO

∽ Rapunzel ∾

13th of Augustus

There has got to be a way to break the witch's hold over Steven, and I shall find it. I shall not eat or sleep until I do. I pin up my hair (a job that takes longer and longer each morn) and pace the room, sticking close to the walls. At first this makes me dizzy, but soon I adjust and can almost do it with my eyes closed. I say *almost* because I tried and walked straight into the wall. My nose is now scraped and there is a spot on my chin that will not stop bleeding. The one positive thing to come out of the experience is that when I looked in the mirror to check my wounds, I learned that my pimple is gone.

For the first time, Steven does not wait for me either to sleep or to stand by the window before he brings me my meal. He swoops down on his rope, with the tray balanced on the tips of his fingers. Before I can even say good afternoon, he places the tray on my table and slithers back up the rope. Before meeting him, I did not know that anything other than a snake could slither. I shall add that to the list of things I used to think were impossible. It is getting to be quite a long list.

While the cold duck and potato soup is inviting, I turn my back on it. I am serious about not eating until I come up with a solution that will lead to our freedom. Hunger sharpens the mind.

MIDDAY

Contrary to my previously held belief, hunger does NOT, in fact, sharpen the mind. What it does is make your belly growl and your senses dull. As the hours creep by, I can no longer smell the food. As a result of my refusal to eat, Sir Kitty ate more than her share and I was forced to use one of my precious pieces of vellum to clean up the mess when her stomach lost its contents. After that, I was no longer hungry.

EVENING

Besides my ban on eating and sleeping today, I have not allowed myself to gaze out the window, nor to use my soap. As a result, by the time the sun disappears in the west, I am feeling woozy, bored, hot, and smelly. I am no closer to figuring out a plan than I was when I awoke this morn.

"Why are you not eating?" Steven asks me, jarring me out of my haze. That man can really sneak up on a person! "Was the food not to your liking?" His face is crinkled in concern.

"No, it's not the food," I assure him. "I am simply direct-ing all of my energy to finding a way for us to escape."

Steven shakes his head at me. "Do not waste your time," he says. "What will happen will happen." With a flick of his wrist he lights a match and holds it to the lamp wick until it catches. He picks up my tray and is about to say good-bye when he sees my bleeding chin. He lifts the lamp from the table and holds it up to get a better look. "What happened to your face? You are all scratched and bleeding. Was it the cat?" His brows furrow as he looks around for Sir Kitty as though she might still have the blood under her nails.

"Of course not," I tell him. "I merely had an accident with the wall."

His face relaxes again and I can see the twitches of a smile on his lips. "Do you want to tell me about it?"

"Truly, no."

"All right, then. Let me put some of your ointment on it, and that will curtail the bleeding." I hand him the tin and he applies a thick layer of ointment to my chin. His touch is surprisingly gentle. For a moment, my eyes water as I remember Mother and Father bandaging a knee or elbow. It feels so long since I was hugged good night or tucked into bed with a kiss on my forehead for sweet dreams. I blink away the tears before they can fall.

"Remember," Steven says as he replaces the lid of the

ointment, "what will happen will happen. One must accept one's fate." With that, he slithers up the rope and is gone.

He is correct. What will happen WILL happen. But that does not mean that I cannot MAKE it happen. I do not believe in fate. Father told me we all make our own destinies, and I plan on having one that does NOT include growing old inside this tower.

Holding on to the walls with my left hand, I continue to circle the room as I think and ponder and question. I discard one plan after another. My best one involves getting Steven to eat some of my food with the sleeping powder in it, then dragging him down the stairs to freedom. But even if I could possibly achieve the first part, that still does not explain how I would get up to the attic in the first place. I could never climb farther than a few feet on that rope, and I certainly could not do it while carrying Steven over my shoulder. All of this thinking gives me a headache and I lean my forehead against the cool wall and close my eyes for a few minutes. When I get out of here, I shall do nothing but gaze at lovely daisies and orchids all day long. I shall eat nothing but almond pies with jelly.

I may be starting to hallucinate because of the hunger, but after a few more circles around the room, I gradually become aware of a wooden bathtub in the center of the rug, with a white towel folded next to it. I stagger up to it and rap on the side with my knuckles. It truly IS a wooden bathtub! I reach over the top and slowly lower my hand, hoping against hope. YES!! There is warm water in there! Steven must have been heating water for this all day!

I tilt my head back and call up to the ceiling, "Thank you, Steven!" I don't get a response, but I don't expect to. I fish around the trunk and pull out the bag with the soap in it. In one fluid move, I pull off my dress, toss it on the floor, and climb into the tub with the soap. Ahhhh. I lean back and close my eyes. At home, Mother rushes me in and out of the tub so everyone can have a turn. But I finally have found something positive about being the only person in the room — the tub is ALL MINE. I can feel my muscles relaxing in the warm water, soaking the day's troubles away. The soap is bubbling up around me. My brain is finally starting to wind down after all the pacing and thinking. I even catch myself humming a tune Mother and I used to sing sometimes as we scrubbed the plates after supper. I splash the water in tune and begin to sing:

Oh, she was a lovely lass, don't ya know,
With a round plump face and a rosy glow,
And wherever she went the gents went, too,

For she always said, why marry one when you can marry a few?

Mother said Grandmother taught her that song and many others when she was a girl. They were not as well off as we are, and Grandmother said that singing always cheered her up, no matter how bad the situation. This song was Mother's favorite, even though she said that any woman who wanted more than one husband had ale head, for one husband to look after was more than enough.

I sing the song once more, then begin to lather up. It takes a few minutes of scrubbing to wash off all the grime that has accumulated since my imprisonment. The water quickly turns gray, then black. Mother would faint if she saw this, but I feel almost like myself again. A hungry version of myself, but myself nonetheless. Before the dirt has a chance to latch back onto me, I stand up and dry myself with the towel. It is a good thing that my hair is under some sort of bewitchment that keeps it lustrous and golden besides causing it to grow, because truly it would have taken hours to wash it, and rebraiding it would take more energy than I could possibly muster right now. I slip one of the last clean dresses over my head and search for the armholes. Suddenly, in a rush of words and images, it comes to me. I stop moving, the dress stuck over my face. I KNOW HOW

TO BREAK THE WITCH'S BOND WITH STEVEN! Even though I am twelve now and too old for such behavior, I jump up and down with glee. Of course, it is generally better to do this when not temporarily blinded by a dress over your face, a lesson I quickly learn as I fall forward and nearly launch myself headfirst into the black water.

CHAPTER TWENTY-THREE

← Prince Benjamin →

14th of Augustus

One more day until the hunt. Father suggested I practice shooting arrows into bales of hay, and I had to eagerly obey so as not to raise suspicion. So far, while aiming squarely at the hay, I have narrowly missed two ducks who were innocently floating in the pond, one lady-in-waiting out for a stroll with a squire, and the village cobbler, who has come to make Annabelle her first pair of leather-soled shoes.

I am truly hopeless. Andrew assures me the men will be too busy worrying about who will bag the biggest stag to bother with me. I hope he is right. Our whole plan depends on it.

CHAPTER TWENTY-FOUR

⁓ Rapunzel ⌒

14ᵗʰ *of Augustus*

I tried to keep my eyes open throughout the night so that when Steven came to collect the tub, I could share my new plan. At one point in the night, I actually had to use my fingers to hold my eyelids open. Alas, I must have succumbed to sleep even without my daily dose of sleeping powder, because the squawking of the birds has just awakened me. The tub is gone, Sir Kitty is playing with the scab on my chin, and it is almost dawn. With a sigh, I blow out the lamp and store it away in the trunk. Before my imprisonment, I saw this time of early morn only during harvest time with Father. Who will help him this year if I am not back? I shake the thought out of my head. I will be back. I have to be!

Belly growling, I pick up Sir Kitty and we go to the window to watch the birds soar over the dew-covered treetops. Soon the last stripes of pink and orange in the east have been burned off by the sun's glow. No doubt as thirsty as I am, Sir Kitty has discovered she can lick the dew off the window ledge. As I stroke her back, her fur suddenly stands on end and her ears flatten. That can't be good.

"You have been busy," a voice cackles from behind me. It is not the voice I had hoped to hear.

My heart begins to pound. What does she mean by that? Has she found out that I know about Steven? Clutching Sir Kitty so tightly she mews in protest, I slowly turn around to face the witch. She is standing in front of my cottage on the wall. She spits onto one of her gnarled fingers and wipes it across the scene, smudging the drawing as she goes. I cringe but refuse to cry out. After all, I have a plan now that will bring me back to the real cottage. I put Sir Kitty down and she runs under the wool blanket. I would, too, if I could. The smell from the pot of meat pie the witch left on the table draws me like bees to a honeysuckle shrub. Truly my mouth is watering. Garlic and mustard fill the room till I feel almost faint from it.

When the witch is done ruining my sketch, she turns and peers right into my face. My body tenses, but I do not move. She gives me a slow once-over and I try to keep my heart from leaping out of my chest. It occurs to me that after my bath I must look quite changed.

"Hmm," she says, tapping one finger against her long,

square chin. If I weren't so terrified, I would laugh, because the finger she is tapping with is the one covered in ash from my drawing. She is making quite a mess of her face. "You look different somehow. I cannot place it." She continues to look, even asking me to turn around. As I turn, I see out of the corner of my eye that Steven is slithering silently down the rope. I am glad I am now facing the other way, because I am sure my expression would give him away. Why is he risking the journey? For one brief second, I wonder if he is going to sneak up on the witch and toss her out the window.

The witch barks at me to turn back and face her. As I do, I see Steven climbing back up the rope. In one hand he is gripping the towel I had used to dry from my bath. *Hurry, Steven, hurry*, I plead silently. He just has time to reach the top and pull up the rope before the witch turns around.

"What are you looking at?" she demands, whirling back to face me.

"Noth . . . nothing," I stammer, quickly returning my gaze. "The cat startled me, that is all."

"I expect your full attention, young Rapunzel. Or I will be only too happy to clear this room of distractions."

"Yes, witch," I say, then hurry to correct myself before her glare deepens. "I mean, yes, Mother Gothel."

"Your sleep," she says, her voice taking on a lilting quality that on anyone else might be considered pleasing. "I trust it has been deep?"

"Yes, Mother Gothel."

"And your meals, they have been satisfactory?"

"Oh, yes, Mother Gothel. Very much so."

"So you would agree that your accommodations have been good?"

I know by now what she wants to hear. "Um, yes?"

She grins widely, and her broken and stained teeth almost make me gag. "I knew you would be happy here. I never had a child of my own before, you see. My line of work is, shall we say, solitary." She cackles like she has just told a joke, then starts to cough. I turn my head as the green phlegm flies from her mouth and lands on the front of her black cape. Charming.

I do not have anything to add, so I keep silent. Where the witch is concerned, silence has proven best.

She continues. "One of these days, you and I shall have a lovely chat about your future. You won't be attending school anymore, of course, so there will be plenty of time for you to learn how to hem my clothes, clean my shoes, and so forth. Yes, we have much to discuss."

I can keep quiet no longer and blurt, "What do you

mean, I will not be attending school anymore? My parents told me that an educated woman is a rare jewel."

The witch throws back her head and laughs. I truly hate it when she does that. I cross my arms and wait for her to stop.

"I am your only parent now," she says, jabbing her finger at my chest. "And the only rare jewel I care to own is one I can wear around my neck. Now go to the window and mind my words. You have one future ahead of you, and it is mine."

My mouth set in a straight line, I march to the window, stamping my feet as I go. I cannot think of a more horrid future than the one she's described. I count to ten, turn around slowly to confirm the witch has gone, and run to the table. I set the sardines and milk down on the floor, and Sir Kitty pops her head out from under the blanket. She nearly trips over her little legs jumping off the "bed." I barely taste the meat pie as it passes my lips. I am sure Steven took extra care with it, because the smell of the herbs wafts through the air as I eat. The tray is now empty except for the lid of the pot. I lift the lid off the tray to place it on top of the empty pot, and as I do, something green catches my eye. In the spot where the lid had been rests a small plate of mint jelly and a tiny silver spoon. Steven must have hidden this from the witch with the lid! I pick up the spoon and am surprised at its weight. This is surely a valuable piece. I peer closer and see a tiny letter S on the handle and wonder if Steven made this himself. I am now so used to eating with wooden utensils and keeping watch for splinters that I am not sure which is the bigger treat, the jelly or the spoon. I take the time to savor each bite. Everything tastes better when eaten with a silver spoon given by a new friend.

MIDDAY

I had fully expected Steven to appear once the witch was gone from the tower. But by the time I finish the mint jelly, he still has not come. I put the tray in the middle of the rug with the silver spoon on top, hoping that might signal him somehow. I gaze up at the trapdoor, but it does not move. I sit back down on the chair, drum my fingers against the tabletop, and wait some more. And then some more after that. I had no idea time could move so slowly. Now more than ever, I realize I must leave this place as soon as possible. I do not think I would make a very good shoeshine girl. I do not wish to find out.

EVENING

The sun has set. The moon is only a thin shard tonight and the tower room is dark. I am still waiting. My empty tray is still sitting on the rug. I do not know why Steven has forsaken me without even hearing my plan.

LATER THAT EVENING

I have fallen asleep in my chair twice now and each time smacked my head on the hard tabletop. At this rate I shall knock myself senseless, and then where will I be? I push back the chair and open my trunk. Pushing aside the dresses, I lift out the lamp, matches, ink, a quill, and my last sheet of vellum.

I light the lamp and set everything up at the table. I dip the quill in the ink and get ready to write what will be the most important letter of my life thus far.

Dear Steven,
I have much to thank you for this eve:
1. The tub.
2. For retrieving the towel before the witch found it.
3. The use of your silver spoon. It is a very special spoon.
I also have much to tell you. I have figured out a way for you to end your servitude to the witch without breaking your bargain with her. We can both free ourselves from her bonds. PLEASE come down so that I can explain everything. We must act soon. I fear she may be getting suspicious.
With much sincerity and appreciation,

Your friend Rapunzel, tower prisoner (hopefully not for too much longer)

I leave the note faceup on the tray so he will be sure to see it right off. I clean up, bring the lamp closer to the "bed," and settle down to wait. Again.

CHAPTER TWENTY-FIVE

← Prince Benjamin →

15th of Augustus

Three valets are dressing me for the hunt. Why they think I am old enough to carry a weapon but not old enough to dress myself is one of life's great mysteries. Out of the corner of my eye, I can see Andrew running across the Great Lawn. It was his job to hide a satchel filled with tomatoes a few feet off the riding path in the forest. He looks up and raises his left hand to signal the job has been completed. From here on, it's all up to me.

"Don't you look handsome," Mum says, entering my chambers as the valets bow and take their leave. Her eyes mist over as she examines me. "So grown up."

From the inside out I am wearing: a thin cotton undershirt, a shirt made of chain mail, a thick woolen tunic, red riding britches, black boots, a leather armband to protect my forearm from the twang of the bow, and a little tin helmet that comes to a point about four inches above my head. Over this my riding cloak is fastened. I can barely move my upper body because of the little loops of metal from the chain mail shirt. How those little loops can weigh nearly twenty pounds is beyond me. The mail and the super-thick tunic will protect my upper body in case one of the animals I'm supposed to be shooting decides that I am the prey and attacks. Even though my outfit is uncomfortable, I admit I feel better facing the troll now.

Still misty, Mum reaches over and straightens my hat. Her left hand is wrapped in a linen bandage, and she is careful not to touch anything with it.

"Mum," I ask as she circles me, patting and pulling on various parts of my outfit, "why did you reach into the fire like that? Annabelle can always get more dolls."

She doesn't answer for a moment, and I wonder if I've offended her somehow. Mum can be quite sensitive. Then she says, "Instinct, I suppose. Had I stopped to think first, I should have been more cautious. Those dolls —" her voice breaks for a second and then starts up again, softer. "Those dolls used to be mine. My mother gave them to me, and her mother had given them to her. I had always believed Annabelle would give them to her own daughter one day. But now, well, that is not to be." She gives one final tug on my cloak to make sure it's secure and stands back. "There. Now you're ready to join the rest of the men. They are planning their strategy by the stables."

Wow. Mum just called me a man. I could join the rest of

the *men*, she said. I practice my kingly stride all the way to the stable, where the groom has my trusty white stallion saddled and ready to go. (Okay, so my trusty steed is not so much a *stallion* — more like a pony who never grew into to a full-size horse. Still, he and I go way back and I wouldn't trade him for anything, even though he and I are almost the same height now. His name, embarrassingly enough, is Snowflake. He already had that name when Father bought him. I have tried in vain over the years to rename him something more manly, like Samuel or Zeus or Montefeur, but he will respond only to Snowflake. I hope none of the men on the hunt find out.)

Elkin is already atop his horse when I arrive. The tailor must have made him a special riding outfit, because it fits him perfectly. He actually looks quite regal on his horse, a reddish-brown mare named Dusty Rose. Up there, he is not quite as froglike. He watches as I slip my foot into the stirrup, then swing my leg over Snowflake's back. The groom attaches my bow to the saddle and hands up a basket of arrows. I strap the basket onto my back so the arrows are accessible if I reach over my shoulder. Not that I plan on accessing them. The other men — some whom I recognize as friends of my father's or royal archers — are also on their horses, talking in a circle. The hunting dogs dart in and out of the horses' legs, clearly excited to get under way. Father sees us and waves us over.

Andrew and I have decided that the best strategy will be to alert Elkin of my plan right before the hunt, when he won't have much time to try to sabotage it. But we are only a few yards from the group, and Elkin is moving steadily forward without so much as a glance in my direction. I pick up my reins and swing Snowflake around to follow. Normally by now Elkin would have slung an insult or two my way. He hasn't even asked if Snowflake has been invited to the spring ball yet, which is his favorite way of insulting my horse's manhood. Instead, he is staring straight ahead. As we get closer to the circle, I notice he is even paler than usual and looks a bit sickly, as he did after learning of his engagement.

I pull Snowflake right up next to him and ask, "Are you feeling all right?"

He nods haltingly, still not meeting my eyes. "I'm fine. Just leave me be."

"Believe me," I mutter, "I would if I could."

We approach the circle, and the men back up their horses to allow us in. Father begins a grand speech, but I am too busy rehearsing what I will say to Elkin to pay much attention. I hear phrases like *the hunt makes the man, the man does not make the hunt; divide and conquer; slow and steady; eye on the prize.* Finally he stops talking and the hunt master raises his horn to his mouth and pauses, looking around dramatically. At last he gives one short blow, then a longer one. The horses neigh loudly as the men dig in their heels and take off, followed by the yapping dogs. I lag behind, trotting instead of galloping. Elkin will not slow down, though, so I still cannot talk to him. The men have thundered into the forest now. I do not understand how they could sneak up on any unsuspecting prey when they are loud enough to rouse the dead.

Elkin finally pulls up on Dusty Rose's reins and comes to a complete halt only a few feet into the forest. Relieved, I catch up. "Listen," I tell him. "Before we go any farther, there is something I need to tell you."

"Snowflake doesn't have a date for the ball?" he asks. But something in the way his says it reveals he is not truly interested in his joke. This is definitely not normal Elkin behavior. But I don't have the time to find out what's going on with him.

"You can insult my horse later, but bide me now."

He finally turns to face me. "What is it? We're going to lose the others."

In a rush I tell him the whole story. I start with meeting Other Benjamin and his father, then on to the bandits and the treasure and finally the troll and how I plan to vanquish him and share the treasure with Other Benjamin so his father can become the Spectacle Maker he was born to be. I even tell him he is welcome to half of my portion. Then I hold my breath and wait for his response.

To my great surprise, the color returns to his cheeks and he laughs. "I was hoping for a miracle to keep me from having to hunt today. I never thought it would be a troll!"

"But . . . but you said you couldn't wait to get in there and bag your supper!"

"I was merely trying to impress your father," he replies.

As I stare at him in shock, he laughs again and says, "What are we waiting for? Let's go get those tomatoes!"

CHAPTER TWENTY-SIX

❧ Rapunzel ❧

15th of Augustus

Once again, morning has greeted me without my having had any awareness of sleep. I hurry to stash away the lamp in case the witch decides to make another surprise visit. My tray is gone and in its place is a tin cowbell and a note with the words, "Ring the bell. I will be there." I quickly ring the bell, and the clonking sound reverberates through the room. The trapdoor swings open and the rope drops. I barely have time to put the bell on the table before Steven reaches the bottom. He sits down on the rug and I join him.

"What happened to you yesterday?" I ask, trying not to sound as hurt as I feel. "I waited for you all day and night."

"My dear Rapunzel, you are right in your note that the witch is getting suspicious. She kept me with her all day long, gathering more ingredients for the sleeping potion and who knows what else. I will listen to your plan, but I have told you my situation and it is irreversible."

"Yes, I know. But when you hear what I have to say, you may feel differently."

He looks doubtful, but I rush ahead.

"First tell me this: Had you ever seen that kind of bug before? The one that your son swallowed?"

He scratches his bald head for a moment and then says, "No, I don't believe I have."

"And when you said the Great Forest was quiet like after a rain, had it actually rained that day?"

He stops to think, then shakes his head.

I continue. "Is it possible the witch was the only person in sight because she scared everyone else away?"

He wrinkles his brow. "I suppose that is possible."

I lean forward. "Steven, I have seen one of those giant flying bugs before. It was the day the witch showed up at my home to take me away. Three of them were flying around her head, but she didn't shoo them away like anyone else would have. I believe the witch set you up from the very beginning. She handpicked you for your skills. She waited until you and your son were alone in the tunnels and then commanded one of those bugs to fly in his mouth. She knew you would run out into the open, and she made sure she was the only person you could go to for help. You are not truly in her debt at all."

I hold my breath as I watch his expression change. It goes from doubt, to uncertainty, to consideration, to acceptance, and finally lands on fury. His green skin turns a deep purple.

"You are right," he says, his voice shaking with anger. "She set me up. I owe her nothing." He sits rock-still, seething. I am slighty afraid he will explode into tiny green pieces. Who knows if his species explodes when angered to such a degree?

I reach out and touch his arm. "Are you going to be all right?"

"All this time away from my family for nothing," he says in measured tones.

"You can go home tonight, Steven. We both can."

He leaps to his feet and starts pacing. "I believe something escaped your notice," he says.

"What do you mean?"

"Think about it, Rapunzel. If the witch set me up, she set you up, too."

"But I am here because of a deal she made with my parents."

"Exactly," he says, extending his hand and helping me stand. "Out of the blue, your mother suddenly craved rampion more than anything in the world, right? Even though she knew the only place to find it was the witch's garden, which was off-limits. She did not consider your father's safety by making him steal it, nor the welfare of the babe she was carrying, even though she had prayed for years to be with child. Now tell me: Is your mother the type of woman who would ever do such a thing?"

I stare at him for a moment, going over his words in my head. I can hear Mother clapping when I sewed my first pillow, and laughing when I tried to cook my first meal and wound up putting so much pepper in the roast that Father sneezed until the sun came up the next day. I can see her crying in anguish when the witch dragged me away. I have been blind to the truth this whole time.

"No!" I tell Steven, my voice rising. "My mother would never have put me or Father in harm's way. Mother was bewitched! I am such a fool!" I fall to the floor and bury my head in my hands. All this time I thought my parents were to blame, when they were duped as much as I.

"Come, Rapunzel," Steven says, kneeling at my side. "Pack up your trunk. It is time to take our leave of this place."

In a daze, I do as he says. It takes only a moment to pack my meager belongings. I tuck a sleepy Sir Kitty into my dress pocket and stand back as Steven carries the trunk up to the attic with him, and then returns for me. He lifts me off the ground as if I weigh no more than a goose feather. When we reach the attic, I see what a dreary place it is. At least the tower room has a window. He hurries me over to the stairs and grabs his own oil lamp to light our way down the dark staircase. The stairs twist around in a spiral, and I am dizzy by the time he pushes the bottom door open. The warm breeze is the first thing to greet us. The second, about to step foot into the clearing, is the witch! Her gaze has not alighted on us yet, but it is only a matter of seconds.

"Run!" I tell Steven, pushing him away from me and grabbing my trunk from his hands.

"I will not leave you behind," he insists.

"We must run in opposite directions. She cannot catch us both! Your family needs you. Go to them and hide where she cannot find you. I will figure out another way."

He hesitates, and in that second, the witch sees us and starts running wildly toward the tower.

"Please, Steven," I implore him. "Leave now, or both of us are doomed!"

"I will never forget you, Lady Rapunzel," he says, kicking up a trail of dust as he runs into the forest toward home.

"Nor I you," I reply to the wind.

I do not bother to run. There would be no point.

The witch is upon me in seconds, dragging me by the hair up the stairs. I am too exhausted to protest. Thankfully, Sir Kitty remains silent and hidden deep in my pocket. I am sure in her wrath the witch would not look kindly upon her. When we reach the open trapdoor in the attic, she tosses my trunk through it and I hear it crash to the floor below. I will not be surprised if she tosses me next. Tightening her grip on my hair, she says, "You are a stupid, stupid girl. I shall have to lock these doors, now that you know of the stairs. Who will feed you now?"

I had thought MY PARENTS would feed me now. I had never planned on darkening the witch's doorstep again. But I am too miserable to answer her. I may never speak again.

"Off with you," she says, fire in her eyes. She pushes me toward the trapdoor and I grab on to the rope and wrap my ankles around it like I have seen Steven do. It takes me much, much longer to reach the bottom, and when I do, my hands are raw from the rough twine. As I step over to my trunk, I feel a whoosh of air followed by a thump behind me. The witch has cut the rope.

"Now throw it out the window," she commands.

All the fight now gone from me, I drag the rope to the window and push it out.

I am truly trapped now.

CHAPTER TWENTY-SEVEN

← Prince Benjamin →

15th of Augustus

I am still in disbelief as I lead our horses to where Andrew stashed the tomatoes. This is not the Elkin I thought I knew. He now has a big grin on his face and is humming the tune the jester was singing the night we got caught. I am pleased by this turn of events, but I still do not fully trust him and will be watching him carefully. As we ride, I glance back and see him take the basket of arrows off his back and tie it to his saddle. I follow suit, and also stash my hat and cloak inside one of the saddlebags. Ah, much better.

"There it is," Elkin sings out, pointing to a tree a few feet to our right. Andrew has hung the satchel on a low tree branch so I will not have to dismount. He is very thoughtful that way. I plan on giving him what is left of my portion of the treasure after Elkin takes his share. I shan't be needing it. Not that Elkin would, either, but somehow I doubt he would be so quick to give it away.

I grab the satchel off the branch and am surprised at how light it is. I reach inside and pull out a paltry four tomatoes. There were supposed to be THREE TIMES that number. I reach in again and pull out a note from Andrew. With my back to Elkin, I read the note:

> *Prince, the garden was bare of tomatoes. I had to beg the head cook to give me these. I told him you and Elkin had to use them as target practice before the hunt. Sorry I could not provide more. Good luck! Your friend and loyal page, Andrew.*

My first thought is to call the whole thing off. The book said that one tomato reaching its target would be enough to fell the troll, but it would give us little room for error.

"Do hurry," Elkin says. "We do not know how long the hunters will remain in the forest."

He is right. It is now or never. I stick the tomatoes into a saddlebag and hang the empty satchel back on the tree. The empty bag is the signal Andrew came up with to let him know the plan is under way.

"Ahem," Elkin says, holding out his hands.

"Yes?"

"Aren't you going to give me some of those?"

"You're actually going to help me fight this troll?" I ask as I reach in and grab two of them.

"I am," he says, accepting the overripe tomatoes and thrusting them in his own saddlebag. "Now which way?"

I take a minute to get my bearings, and then gesture off to the left. I can still hear the hunters galloping and whooping in the other direction. With all the noise they are making, it's a wonder we ever see meat on our table.

CHAPTER TWENTY-EIGHT

⌒ Rapunzel ⌒

15th of Augustus

My trunk is a mess. Between the broken ink bottle and the oil from the shattered lamp, everything is coated with a black goo. I did pull one item from the trunk unharmed — Steven's silver spoon. He must have shoved it in there when I was not looking. He is sneaky that way. I miss him already. Sure, he was smaller than my father — and greener, of course — but he was the closest thing I had to one in this place. Even though I am back here, I am glad that he is home where he belongs.

CHAPTER TWENTY-NINE

↞ Prince Benjamin ↠
15th of Augustus

After a few minutes, we find ourselves on what must once have been a riding path but is now so overgrown it is hard to recognize as one. The horses have to step carefully to avoid fallen vines and branches. We ride steadily for a few miles until we come upon the large oak tree that signifies we are only a mile or so away from the cave. The rest of the journey will be more treacherous, for we must turn away from the path, with only the trees themselves to guide us. It is cool this deep in the forest, but my thick tunic keeps me comfortable.

"Uh, are you sure this is the right way?" Elkin asks from behind me. The brush is so thick, there is room for only one horse at a time.

"I think so," I answer honestly. "I have memorized the markings that should guide us. See this tree here? It has a slash of red ochre on the trunk. That tells me we are to turn right."

"Who made these markings?" he asks, reaching his hand out to trace the design with his finger.

I shrug. "The bandits, I guess. Before Father cleared them out of the forest."

"You are sure they're gone, right?"

"Andrew says they are."

"Oh, well, if *Andrew* says so, then I'm sure it must be true."

"What do you have against him, anyway?"

"Forget it — just keep looking for those signs. If we get lost here, no one will find us for days."

I am tempted to reply that his hair would be the only beacon our rescuers would need, but I hold my tongue. For better or worse, we are partners now. We continue to ride in silence, finding marking after marking. I only miss one, and that's because a bluebird is sitting on a branch in front of the mark. We wind up finding a small brook where the horses can refresh themselves with a drink. Judging from the position of the sun above us, it is already well past noontime. We have to hurry.

Once we are back on track, it is not long before we close in on our target. I bring Snowflake to a halt and Elkin squeezes up beside us. "We are almost there," I whisper. "I think we should dismount and tie the horses here. That way we will be better able to sneak up on the troll."

I expect Elkin to argue, but he only nods and quietly swings himself off Dusty Rose. I join him on the ground and we tie the horses to a tree. We carefully transfer the tomatoes to our pockets.

"When we get there," I instruct Elkin, "follow my lead. Hopefully we can approach from behind so the element of surprise will be on our side. I had expected to have many more tomatoes, so aim carefully."

Elkin nods, and we creep in the direction of the cave. It is so well hidden that we almost miss it. Elkin tugs at my tunic and points it out to me. The cave is no more than an opening in the rock face of a hillside. A fire pit is smoldering in a small clearing out front. The troll must have just finished his lunch. I wonder where it fell on the long list of options between berry and horse. I put my fingers to my lips, and we both take out our tomatoes and tiptoe forward. To my ears, each crunch of a fallen leaf sounds as loud as the hunt master's horn.

I motion for Elkin to stand at the left side of the entrance, and I take post on the right. With my back against the hard rock, I peer inside but can see nothing but darkness. Neither of us suggests going in, so we just stand there, looking around. My heart is beating so loud and hard, I am certain Elkin can hear it.

After what seems like an eternity (but is probably only

ten minutes), we hear a rustling in the cave and both instinctively back away.

"Get ready," I whisper, feeling the weight of the tomatoes in each hand.

"All ri . . . right," Elkin stutters. He is pale again, but he's not backing down.

The rustling is getting louder. The troll is definitely about to come out.

"On the count of three," I whisper.

Its shadow has now crossed the threshold. The shadow looks big. And hairy!

"One . . . two . . . three. NOW!"

At that moment the troll emerges from the cave into the sunlight. With matching war cries, we both fire off our tomatoes. Amazingly, all four are direct hits. The troll should now fall down dead. If only it *were* a troll.

We have just assaulted an old hermit!

CHAPTER THIRTY

∽ Rapunzel ∾
15th of Augustus

I have gone to the window to stare out at the world that I was so close to being a part of again. To have been so close and to have failed has left me empty. My belly is rumbling so loud, I am certain the blackbirds can hear it. A yellow-beaked jackdaw tries to land on the same branch as a red-horned owl, and I watch as the owl flaps its wings in warning. Out of the corner of my eye I see movement below the tower. For a second my heart leaps, thinking it is Steven, although I know it cannot be. It is the witch, of course, and she is holding a bowl in her arms.

"Are you hungry, my dear daughter?" she calls up, all sweetness and light.

Every inch of me cringes when she calls me *dear daughter*. I still cannot bear to speak to her. But I am very hungry. With a sigh, I nod my head.

"Then let down your hair and I shall climb up and feed you." She tilts the bowl so I can see round red objects that must be berries. At this point I would eat the bark off a tree.

While I am thinking about filling my belly, her words finally sink in. I have suddenly found my voice.

I lean out the window and yell, "Did you say to let down my HAIR? And you will use it to CLIMB UP?"

"Yes, dear daughter."

"But it is not nearly long enough, and I would fall from the window," I point out. "Surely your weight is too much for me to bear."

"Do as I say, dear child. Unwrap your hair, and you will find it is both long enough and strong enough to do the task at hand."

Certain that she is madder than I already know her to be, I begin to unwrap my braid. Whole minutes go by and I am still unraveling it. I step to the window and lower the braid. To my shock, it really DOES reach the ground. The witch latches on and begins to climb. She moves very quickly, nearly as quickly as Steven climbed up the rope. I can feel her weight, but no more than if it were Sir Kitty swinging on it. The witch reaches the window ledge and I back up to let her in.

She dusts herself off and hands me a heavy pewter bowl. To my surprise, there are no red berries, only twigs. I look up at her with raised brows.

She laughs in that way that I hate. I realize I have been tricked.

"Did you truly believe you would be rewarded for your disloyal behavior? You shall go hungry today to think about what you've done."

My head sinks to my chest. The witch snatches the bowl from my hands and then climbs onto the window ledge. My hair is still hanging out of the window. She grabs hold of it and lowers herself down. Once again I feel only the lightest tug. When she reaches the bottom she waves up at me. "Ta-ta, my daughter. See you in the morn."

This is easily the lowest point of my time here.

CHAPTER THIRTY-ONE

← Prince Benjamin →

15ᵗʰ of Augustus

Too stunned to say anything, we stare wide-eyed at the old man as the tomato pulp rolls down his long beard and ragged clothes. He reaches up and parts his long hair so he can see us better. Elkin and I are both frozen in our boots.

"Well," says the not-a-troll-but-a-hermit in a cracking voice that clearly hasn't been used in some time. "What a lovely greeting."

I force my mouth to work. "We . . . we are deeply sorry, sir. Truly, we thought you were a troll."

Elkin nods his head vehemently. "We were told — well, *he* was told — that a troll would be guarding a cave full of treasure."

The old man wipes the juice off his face with his sleeve and squeezes out his beard. Then, of all things, he chuckles, and his mouth forms a sort of half smile.

"Ah, so that old rumor is still going strong," he says, shaking his head. "All these years. Amazing."

Elkin and I exchange a look. "Rumor?" I ask with a sinking feeling. "There is no troll? No bandit treasure?"

The hermit shakes his head. Tomato seeds fly out and land in the dirt.

My heart sinks. All my grand plans for Other Benjamin and his father flit past my eyes. There goes my last chance to be immortalized in song. "But the map, the book. They all said —"

"Come," the hermit says. "Sit with me and I shall explain." He heads into the cave and clearly expects us to follow.

Elkin grabs my arm. "What if it's a trap? We did just tomato him, you know!"

"We don't have a choice," I reply. "We can't be rude after what we did."

Elkin nods grudgingly and we step into the darkness. Once we are a foot or two inside, candles illuminate the cave fairly well. I can make out a pile of round fruit, a bowl of water, and a bed of straw and feathers covered with wool blankets. Fur pelts line the walls. It is actually quite cozy. Not very roomy, though. With the three of us, there is barely enough space to turn around. The hermit sits down in the center of the cave on a bear pelt, and motions for us to sit, too.

"Can I offer you anything?" he asks. "Ale? Wine?" He

peers closely at us in the murkiness. "No, I see you are not yet old enough for libations. Water, perhaps?"

I shake my head but Elkin says, "Yes, please."

The hermit reaches behind him and dips a small metal cup into the bowl of water. He hands the water to Elkin, who gulps it down. I must admit it does look refreshing. But my throat is too tight to eat or drink anything.

"How long have you been here?" Elkin asks.

"I have lost count," the hermit says. "Since well before either of you were born." As he talks, I notice he is stroking something next to him. A rat? No, a hare. It might be the candlelight playing tricks with my eyes, but I think it has a brown spot on its rump!

"And it was you who started the rumor of the troll?" Elkin asks. My head is spinning too fast to form questions — a problem Elkin does not appear to suffer from.

"Yes," the hermit answers. "I needed to find a way to keep marauders and bandits and even the good king's knights away from my door. I am a very private man, you see."

"I can see that," Elkin says.

"Cat got your tongue, Prince Benjamin?" the hermit says, turning to me. "You are awfully quiet."

"How do you know who I am?" I ask. Due to the tightness of my throat, it comes out squeaky.

Elkin laughs and I hurry to clear my throat.

"Oh, I know many things," the hermit answers cryptically. "One cannot live alone in the forest without picking up a few skills."

"Why *do you* live here?" Elkin asks. "I thought the forest was cleared of hermits at the same time the bandits were all gathered up."

"We hermits are a stubborn lot," the old man says with that strange half smile. "We know how to hide. Come, I'll show you." He stands up, grabs a candle from its niche on the wall, and moves aside one of the fur pelts hanging on the wall. To my surprise, there is another cave behind it. And then another cave behind THAT one. Finally we wind up in a large cavern and I am wishing I had my cloak, because it is very cold in here. The hermit uses his candle to light others all around the room. When my eyes focus, I can't believe what I see before me. The walls of the cave are completely covered in spectacular artwork. Someone has painted pictures of animals playing, men and women dancing, mountains and lakes, and everything under the sun. I turn around in a circle. There is not one inch left uncovered.

"Wow!" Elkin exclaims, echoing my thoughts. "Did you do all this?"

The hermit nods. "This is my life's work. This is why I could not leave." He tells us to take all the time we want, and heads back out. Elkin and I walk around the room, pointing out things to each other and lightly touching the beautiful renderings.

"This is the most amazing place I have ever seen," Elkin says, wiping a tear from the corner of one eye.

I look away out of politeness. Who would have thought that my brutish cousin would be moved by art? Clearly, there is a lot I do not know about him. "I cannot imagine its equal," I say in agreement. "But we'd better go." Even so, it is quite a while before we can drag ourselves away.

CHAPTER THIRTY-TWO

～੭ Rapunzel ੮～

15th *of Augustus*

I watch out the window as the witch disappears behind the tower. Then I pull my hair back in and let it pile up on the floor behind me. What do I do now? I have no vellum to write on, no Steven to commiserate with, and no food. Once again, Sir Kitty has resorted to licking the dew off the walls. I remember what Grandmother said about singing when times were bad. Well, times don't get any badder than this.

I clear my throat a bit and then launch into the songs Mother taught me. I alternate between "The Lovely Lass," "The King of the Wolf People," "Dipsy Doodle," and "Mitsy the Wonder Dog." At first I feel silly and self-conscious, even though the only ones who can hear me are the birds and Sir Kitty. But there is something about having my voice sail out on the breeze over the treetops that is bringing some life back into me.

CHAPTER THIRTY-THREE

← Prince Benjamin →

15th of Augustus

We find the hermit out by the fire pit, sitting on a moss-covered log and puffing away on a pipe. He has changed his clothes. Still rags, but not tomato-covered rags. "What do you think of my work?" he asks.

Elkin answers first. "You could be paid your weight in gold to share your talent with the world. You could have a home, and real clothes. Why hide out here?"

"This is how I like to live," the hermit explains, taking the pipe from his mouth and resting it on his knee. "We all have our place in this world. This is my place."

A sigh escapes me before I can stop it. The old man looks up. "What is it, sire? What troubles you?"

I look down at my feet and figure I might as well tell him the truth. Somehow I imagine he knows it, anyway. "I had hoped to use the bandits' treasure to help a villager to find *his* place. And . . . well . . . I thought maybe someday, some-one somewhere might sing a song about me afterward." I blush as I say that last part, and expect to hear Elkin laugh at me again. When I don't hear anything, I finally look up to meet the hermit's eyes. He is watching me intently. I begin to squirm under his gaze. It is as though he is seeing right through me.

"You will find other ways to help your friend," he tells me. "You have only to use your eyes. As for your song, someone will indeed be singing for you. But you must listen hard for it."

"I'll sing for you, Benjamin," Elkin jokes. "You may not like it, though!"

The hermit smiles his crooked smile and sticks the pipe back in his mouth. "The song I speak of is for Benjamin alone. Yours, young Prince Elkin, is an easier path." And with that, he stands and walks back into his cave without a backward glance. We stand by the fire pit for another minute, not sure what we should do.

"What do you mean, *use my eyes*?" I call into the cave. "What do you mean, *someone will be singing for me*?"

But the only thing that comes out of the cave is silence.

"Well, I guess that's that, then," Elkin says. "We REALLY must go now." When I don't budge, he grabs my arm and drags me back toward the horses.

As we ride back out to the main trail, the hermit's words keep playing in my head over and over, like one of Annabelle's nursery rhymes. How could I hear a song if I'm not listening?

Can one hear and not listen? Has the hermit gone batty from living in that cave for so long?

"Um, Benjamin?" Elkin calls from behind me. "Are you watching for the red marks? I don't remember seeing this grove before."

I snap to attention and turn Snowflake in a circle. Uh-oh. Where are we? Nothing looks familiar to me, either. We try retracing our steps but only wind up in the same spot. I close my eyes and try to remember how far apart the marked trees were from each other. Maybe that will help. With my eyes closed I am aware of Snowflake's breathing. I hear the rustling of the leaves, which means the wind is picking up. I'm about to open my eyes and tell Elkin that it's hopeless, when I hear something else. It sounds like a faint singing. My eyes flutter open. "Did you hear that?"

"Hear what?" Elkin asks, glancing worriedly at the rapidly setting sun.

"It sounded like a girl's voice," I say, twisting around in my saddle. "Wait — there it is again! She's . . . she's singing!"

"Sorry, cousin, but I hear nothing," Elkin says. "Are you certain you're not imagining it?"

I tilt my head . . . and there it is again. I hear a melody riding on the wind, but I cannot make out the words. "I swear by my father's kingdom I am not."

Elkin squeezes his eyes shut and turns one ear up to the

sky, then the other. He opens his eyes again and shakes his head. "Perhaps this is what the hermit meant about hearing someone singing when you listen?"

"But you were just listening — why wouldn't you have heard?"

Elkin shrugs. "Perhaps I am not meant to hear. The hermit said this was your story, not mine. What does the singing sound like?"

I lead Snowflake a few yards to the right, and the singing gets louder. But then it fades again until I back up a few steps. "She sounds — I don't know — sad or something. I think I need to find her, but I cannot tell where the singing is coming from."

Then a loud horn splits the air and we both jump a few inches in our saddles. The horses lift their noses into the air and sniff.

"I know where THAT'S coming from," Elkin says. "The hunt master is announcing the end of the hunt. You'll have to come back tomorrow to find your singing girl."

"Wait — how will I find this spot again?"

Elkin thinks for a minute, then his face lights up. "We can shoot our arrows into the trees as we head back. We won't want to return with a full quiver, anyway, or else the king will know we did not hunt."

"Er . . . I do not know if you have seen me shoot an

arrow, but no rider is safe near me. My arrows have a mind of their own."

"I shall do it," he says, hurrying to detach his bow from his saddle. "You leave your arrows here to help you find the exact spot you first heard the singing."

I do as he says, dumping all of my arrows into a pile at my side. Elkin's first shot easily hits the closest tree with a pleasing twang. Well, sure, when we're not MOVING, even I could have done that. Well, I *probably* could have done that. He swings Dusty Rose around and heads off, shooting arrows as he goes.

I hurry to keep up. "We are still lost, remember?"

Elkin shakes his head. "I have a feeling the horses know how to get back. Let them guide us."

"But how —"

"Just trust me," he says, and drops his reins.

Trusting Elkin. Whoever would have imagined? Not able to think of a better option, I follow suit. A few minutes later I see a tree with a red mark, then another, and another. We are back on the path! Elkin dumps the rest of his arrows in a thick bush. Now able to ride next to each other again, I ask him where he suggests we tell my father we were during the hunt.

"Leave it to me," Elkin says.

"Assuming we are not punished for the rest of our natural lives, how will I get back into the forest to find the girl?"

"Leave that to me, too. Now let's put on our helmets again and rejoin the hunters. Do you hear them up ahead?"

I *do* hear them! The thundering of hooves is getting closer.

"On my mark," Elkin says, picking up the reins and halting his horse. "One . . . two . . . three!" He digs in his heels and Dusty Rose takes off. I follow close behind. Miraculously, we wind up right at the end of the group of hunters, looking for all the world as though we'd been there the whole time.

CHAPTER THIRTY-FOUR

∽ Rapunzel ∾
15th of Augustus

My oil lamp now useless, all I have left are a few matches that managed to escape the ravages of the spilled ink and oil. I light one of them and hold the small mirror up to my face. The glass has shattered, but I can still see into it. My reflection is all jumbled and shadowy. Who is this girl now? Who is Rapunzel? I stare hard into my grass-colored eyes, now splintered in the mirror, and ask the question again: WHO AM I??

I take a deep breath. Out loud, I reply, "I am me. I am a singer of songs. I am my parents' only daughter. I am a friend to my schoolmates and to Steven. I am mother and protector to Sir Kitty. I am not a child anymore." A wave of determination passes through me like a hot wind and even with my empty belly, I feel my strength returning. I am NOT going to let the witch destroy what is inside me. It is all I have left.

CHAPTER THIRTY-FIVE

← Prince Benjamin →

15th of Augustus

When we get out of the forest and back onto the castle grounds, the men slow their horses to a trot. Father hangs back and pulls up alongside us.

"How did you do, boys?" he asks, his face flushed with the thrill of the hunt. There is a stag tied to the rump of his horse. "I see you have used all your arrows. Excellent!"

"Er, thank you, Father," I say uncertainly. "We, uh, did not catch anything, though."

Elkin adds, "Benjamin did a fine job, uncle. He missed a fox by barely an inch!"

Father clasps me on the shoulder. "Fine job, just fine."

I smile weakly. "Er, thanks?" My cheeks are burning, but Father doesn't notice.

"In fact," Elkin continues, "we worked so well together as a pair that I was hoping we could go back tomorrow to try again."

"I don't see why not," Father says, clasping Elkin on the

shoulder this time. "Benjamin's mother will be very pleased that he is finally taking an interest in a sport."

When Father leaves us to bid good-bye to his hunting party, I turn to Elkin and say, "I thought I was supposed to find the singing girl on my own. How shall I do that if you're with me?"

"Do not worry — I won't be with you. I'll have the groom saddle me up and then leave you once we enter the forest. Perhaps I'll visit the hermit again. I kind of liked him."

"I liked him, too," I say.

Elkin adds, "Although he could use a good bathing!"

I laugh as we pull our horses into the stable and dismount. Andrew comes running out to greet us, the empty satchel in his hand. We pull him into the private courtyard and fill him in on what happened. He shakes his head the whole time, repeatedly saying, "I do not believe it! I simply do not believe it!" When we get to the part about hitting the hermit with the tomatoes, his hands fly over his mouth. When we are finished, he says, "What if you found the wrong cave and the real one, with the treasure, and the troll, is still out there?"

"Huh," Elkin and I say together. I hadn't considered that. Then I shake my head. "No, the hermit told us he had started the rumor about the troll and the treasure to be left in peace. We have to face facts. The legend was a lie."

Andrew sinks his head into his hands. "I am so sorry, sire. Forgive me for sending you on a wild-goose chase."

"No, no, Andrew," I tell him, patting him on the back. "It was truly a grand adventure. I have never had one its equal."

"Nor I," Elkin says.

"Besides," I continue, beginning to pace, "the adventure is not over. I have a singing girl to find!"

CHAPTER THIRTY-SIX

∽ Rapunzel ∾

16th of Augustus

Father says that when it rains, the gods are crying. We used to try to make up reasons for their tears. "One of them stubbed his toe!" or "One of them pushed the other off a cloud!" or "One of them proposed marriage to another but she turned him down!" Whatever the reason, there must be a lot of crying going on up there, because it is pouring like the heavens themselves have opened up.

This is the first rain since my imprisonment, and in a way, the pounding on the treetops and the tower walls is soothing. Plus, it offers an endless supply of water. All I need do is stick my head out, lean back, and open my mouth.

I fear the witch will not come because of the rain. I hate the fact that I need her for food. Steven's whole kitchen is right above me, but it might as well be in another country. But come she does, and this time the bowl really contains red berries, with nuts and raisins, too. She scowls at me as I grab for it, but leaves me and Sir Kitty to eat in peace. When we are through (it does not take long, due to the fact that we gobble it down like we have never tasted food before) I continue my singing. Sometimes I make up a new verse about a girl with a dream of freedom. I am quite a talented songwriter, if I do say so myself. Perhaps I will have a new career ahead of me when I leave here.

IF I leave here.

CHAPTER THIRTY-SEVEN

← Prince Benjamin →

16ᵗʰ of Augustus

It is barely dawn when Elkin and I saddle up the horses. Mum is overjoyed that I have taken an interest in a sport, and she made sure that I had the first bite of Father's stag last night at supper. I am still surprised that she is so quick to let us go into the forest by ourselves, but I am certainly not going to press the issue and risk her changing her mind.

We have to make a pretense of packing our bow and arrows, although we will dump the arrows as soon as we enter the forest. Andrew has agreed to go in after us and collect them so no one else will find them first and get suspicious. He also convinced the royal painter to give him a jar filled with yellow ochre so that I can mark the trees as I venture into parts unknown.

Just as the stable boy swings open the gates, the first drop of water hits the ground, followed in quick succession by the second, third, and fourth drops. By the time Elkin and I have led the horses a foot from the gate, it is full-on pouring.

A peal of thunder rumbles overhead and the horses whinny in response. My heart sinks. The groom approaches and says, "I am sorry, sires. I must bring the horses back into the stables. They are not to be ridden in a storm."

I reach down and put my hand on Snowflake's flank. I can feel him shaking slightly. "He'll be fine," I say weakly, not even convincing myself.

"I am sorry, sire, truly," the groom says, holding out his hands for the reins. With a sigh, I hand them over. Elkin does the same. Having no choice, we dismount and run back toward the castle, hunching our shoulders against the rain.

"She'll still be there tomorrow," Elkin assures me as we run across the field.

"You don't know that for sure," I reply. A bolt of lightning shoots across the sky and we pick up our pace.

"That is a chance you will have to take," he calls out from behind. His short legs can't carry him as fast as mine and I slow down to let him catch up. We run together into the main courtyard, which is sheltered from the rain by wooden slats overhead.

"You must cheer up," Elkin says, shaking the water from his hair. "Let me beat you at a game of chess to take your mind off your worries."

It didn't exactly take my mind off my worries, but it *was*

fun beating Elkin three times in a row until Mum said I was being rude to our houseguest and I had to let him win one game.

NEXT DAY, 17TH OF AUGUSTUS

Thankfully, it is bright and sunny this morning and we have gotten an early start. My heart is thudding against my tunic. What if I do not hear the singing again? Perhaps the girl was only out with her family for a day of riding and is long gone. Will my search be in vain?

"Are you certain you'll be all right?" Elkin asks as we reach the area of the forest where we are to part ways. "You are mumbling to yourself in a particularly odd way."

"Your concern is touching," I tell him. "But I'll be fine." I pat the back of Snowflake's head for comfort.

"Just in case," he says, "take this horn and use it if you need help."

"Where did you get this?" I ask, admiring the brass-and-leather horn. It is heavier than I would have thought.

"I borrowed it from the hunt master," Elkin says with a wink as he turns to follow the path to the hermit's cave.

"You *borrowed* it?" I call after him.

"Okay, so I stole it," he calls over his shoulder. "But he won't need it today and you'll make sure I give it back." He laughs as he disappears into the trees. Perhaps Elkin has not totally changed his ways . . . but I *did* notice a big satchel of clothes tied to the back of Dusty Rose's saddle. I have a feeling the hermit will be dressing better soon.

By following Elkin's arrows, which thankfully were not felled by the heavy rains, I easily find the spot where I first heard the singing. With a deep breath, I close my eyes. For a few minutes I do not hear anything but the beating of my heart and the occasional squawk of a bird. Then the wind picks up a bit and I hear the singing, ever so faintly. I am tempted to gallop off in the direction I think it's coming from, but I force myself to do as the hermit said and just listen. Snowflake whinnies, almost like he is trying to tell me something. Can he hear the girl, too? What if I drop his reins and let him find her? Could that possibly work? Well, it wouldn't be any more surprising than all the other things that have happened in the last few days. I drop the reins.

"Okay, Snowflake, let's go find that girl!"

And off he goes! We weave in and out of trees, sometimes hitting an old bridle path, sometimes climbing over logs and under low branches. I break off a thin twig and use the tip to paint a slash of yellow on the tree trunks as we pass. The song is getting louder and louder until I can finally hear the words.

Oh, a dipsy and a doodle and a doodle and a dip,
The maiden drops her bonnet and upon it he does slip,
But he loves her fully anyway and she agrees to wed,
Oh, a dipsy and a doodle and a doodle and a —

As we round the final bend, the song suddenly cuts off. Snowflake comes to a halt just as suddenly and I am thrust forward in my saddle. I strain to listen. Nothing. My chest is tightening up. Have we come this far for nothing? I move Snowflake forward a few feet and see past the trees into a clearing. In the middle is the last thing I thought I would see — a tower as tall as our castle watchtower! Until now, the treetops have restricted it from view. Just below the top of the tower is a small window. I peer closer and see that inside the window stands a girl. I have found the singing girl! She lives in a tower? How strange. I am about to charge forward when a stooped old woman approaches the bottom of the tower. In a cackling voice she says, "Rapunzel, Rapunzel, let down your hair."

A few seconds later, a thick golden braid is lowered from the window all the way down to the grass below. My jaw falls open. How could one girl's hair be that long? Why did the strange woman want her to hang it out the window? Then the most bizarre thing of all happens — the old woman starts CLIMBING UP THE GIRL'S HAIR!!! Hand over hand, she shinnies up at a steady pace. When she reaches the window ledge, the girl backs up and the old woman climbs inside. I rub my eyes. Did I just see what I think I saw? Snowflake paws the ground with his hoof, and whinnies. I back us up a few paces, fearing the woman might not like having company.

I dismount from Snowflake's back, give him some hay to nosh on, and sit on a nearby tree stump to wait. What I am waiting for, I do not know, but I keep my eyes focused solely on that window. After about ten minutes, the girl steps to the window again and I jump to my feet. I'm about to run to the tower when the old lady climbs out onto the ledge and starts sliding down the braid. I shrink back again and hide behind a tree until the woman disappears around the back of the tower.

The girl pulls her hair back inside and does not return to her singing. I wait by Snowflake for a long time, until I am certain the witch is not returning. Then I pace back and forth beneath the tower, unsure what to do. Should I toss a rock in her window to get her attention? That's probably not a great idea, considering my history with anything that requires aim. No doubt I would strike her in the head by mistake. I circle the perimeter of the tower, looking for any way in. On the opposite side from the window I see a door, but it has been sealed up tight with cement. Does the girl never leave the tower? Is she a prisoner there?

I see no other alternative but to climb up the same way as the old woman. I stand under the window, clear my voice, and call out, "Rapunzel, Rapunzel, let down your hair." Truth be told, since my voice hasn't completely changed yet, I don't sound all that very different from the old lady. It works! She lets down her hair! I grab hold of the end of it and pray I am not so heavy that she comes flying out the window. My ascent is not as smooth as the old woman's, and I occasionally bang a knee or elbow against the hard stone wall. When I finally get to the ledge, I swing my leg over and hop in. That is the last thing I remember before waking up some time later on the hard stone floor. The girl with the hair is standing over me, a heavy pewter bowl held firmly in her hands. My head is throbbing and — unless I am going crazy — a cat is licking my ear.

CHAPTER THIRTY-EIGHT

∾ Rapunzel ∾
17th of Augustus

Perhaps I acted a bit rashly. I suppose I could have let the boy speak his peace *before* knocking him out. In my own defense, he HAD tricked me by pretending to be the witch. I am standing over him now, bowl poised to strike again if necessary. Sir Kitty sniffs the boy's clothes, which look very fine and well tailored even to my untrained eye, and is now licking the boy's ear for some reason. When he awakens from his bowl-induced sleep, his eyes slowly open and his hand reaches out to rub the spot on his head where I struck him. His glasses have fallen off his face and are dangling from one broken stem.

"What did you do THAT for?" the boy asks, grimacing. He slowly sits up and leans against the tower wall for support.

How could he ask me that? I had forgotten how dense boys could be. "You just CLIMBED UP MY HAIR! Uninvited, I might add."

"I could not figure out any other way to get in," he says. "This place is locked up tighter than a prison."

"Look around," I tell him. "This IS a prison."

He feels for his glasses and discovers the broken stem. With a deep sigh, he reaches into a pocket inside his cloak and pulls out an extra pair. "These are my last ones," he says, fitting them on his face and looking around at last. "So you are a prisoner, then. I feared as much. You do not look like a very dangerous criminal." He smiles slightly and adds, "Although you know how to wield a salad bowl quite well! You can put it down now. I assure you, I mean you no harm."

I debate my options. Compared to the witch, he does look pretty harmless. I lay the bowl down on the floor and Sir Kitty runs over to check it for milk. Disappointed, she climbs up onto the boy's lap and curls up to sleep.

"Well, my cat seems to like you. Perhaps now you will tell me why you are here?"

"Ladies first," he says. "Tell me why YOU are here."

Might as well get it over with. I sit down a few feet away and tell him my sorry tale. He gasps in all the right places, and even laughs a few times, such as when I tell him how my shoe fell off when I was dangling from the window.

"That is some story," he says, shaking his head. "I did not think such things as witches and little green creatures who live in underground caverns existed anymore."

My face darkens. "Are you saying you don't believe me?"

"Oh, no," he says hurriedly. "Of course, I do."

"Good," I say, relieved. "Or else I might have to hit you with the salad bowl again."

He grins. He has a nice smile. He could use a haircut, but who am I to talk about that? "So now you know who I am, but I do not know your name, nor why you are in my tower."

The boy gently moves Sir Kitty from his lap to the floor, stands up slowly, and bows. He is quite tall for his age. "Prince Benjamin at your service, Lady Rapunzel. I have come to rescue you."

Well! This is an interesting twist in my life's tale. Rescued by a prince! Who would have guessed it?

"But how did you know I was here?" I ask. I feel foolish looking up at him from the floor, so I stand up, too. I am pleased to report that I am only a few inches shorter than he.

"I followed the beautiful singing," he says. "The troll — who turned out to be a hermit — told me to listen for it. The tower is far from Father's castle, but I found you. My horse Snowflake helped, too."

I don't know what to say. "You think my singing is beautiful?"

He blushes. "It's okay, I guess."

I smile. "Now what was that about a troll?"

The prince proceeds to tell me his own story, which is filled with many adventures as well. I am touched that he is risking punishment by sneaking out to find me.

"So what do we do now?" I ask. "I still cannot jump from the window, even if you were to try to catch me below."

"I shall alert the castle guards and they will storm the forest and free you. They will bring a ladder and have you down in no time."

"No, no, you can't do that," I rush to tell him. "The witch is very smart. She will surely be alerted by all the activity in the forest and will take it out on me or my parents. Please, you can't tell the authorities about this."

He begins to pace the room. "But I cannot carry a ladder on horseback — it would not fit. And I have never seen a length of rope that could reach the ground."

"I know!" I say excitedly. "We can MAKE a ladder. I think silk is the only material that would be strong enough. You'd be able to carry that easily. Do you have any silk at the castle?"

"Mum has lots of it. I can ride home and return with it tomorrow."

I nod happily. "If you bring me long pieces, I can tie them together and form knots to help us climb down."

"Your wish is my command," he says, bowing again.

Now it is my turn to blush. "You better leave now. I

don't want to know what would happen if the witch caught you here."

We head over to the window and I lower my braid outside. Climbing onto the ledge, he says, "I hope I am not too heavy."

I shake my head. "My hair is bewitched somehow. I barely feel your weight."

He begins his descent. "I shall see you tomorrow," he calls up. "Be well until then."

"Come around this same time," I reply. "To be sure the witch has left."

When he reaches the bottom, I lean out to watch him ride off on his white horse. The horse looks a little small for him, but I can tell by the way he greeted it that he loves the horse very much. I quickly pull in my braid and go lie down on the "bed" to think over the events of this day. The prince is sort of cute in a tall, gawky kind of way. I don't recall thinking a boy cute before.

I turn on my side and watch the birds fly past the window. Soon I shall be as free as they are. I notice a slight soreness in my cheeks and reach up to touch my face. Ah, I am still smiling — that's what the ache is from!

CHAPTER THIRTY-NINE

⤙ Prince Benjamin ⤚

17th *of Augustus*

I cannot wait to return to the castle to tell Elkin and Andrew what has transpired today. They will NOT believe it. I easily follow the yellow-marked trees back to the path. I stop at the brook to let Snowflake drink and to wait for Elkin. I am anxious to start collecting the silk. Fortunately, Elkin turns up only moments after I do.

"Did you find your singing girl?" he asks, maneuvering Dusty Rose so he can join Snowflake at the brook. "Wait, you do not have to answer. I can see it on your face!"

"What do you mean?"

"Your expression is all dewy and sappy."

"It is not!"

"So tell me the story, then," he says as we move the horses back onto the path.

"I am in a hurry to return home. I'll tell you and Andrew at the same time."

"Fine," he says curtly, and gallops off ahead.

The sun is still high when we reach the stables. I have

never met a girl like Rapunzel. I didn't feel like a clod around her. And she didn't make fun of Snowflake's name when I told it to her. She was smart and funny. Elkin would say that she needed a good bathing, and perhaps that is true. But her green eyes were sharp, and her golden hair glimmered like silk.

We hand the horses over to the groomers and hurry into the castle. Father walks out of his throne room, followed by Andrew and a new page, who are both carrying a pile of ledgers and some maps. The new page is so small he can barely see over the books in his arms. Andrew told me that when he becomes a squire, he will miss being a mentor to the new pages. I'm sure they will miss him, too.

"Hello there, boys!" Father booms, clasping us both on the shoulders. "Walk with me and tell me of your exploits."

Having no choice, we walk down the long hallway to the Great Hall where I see some barons and noblemen are waiting. "Er," I begin, "we don't want to keep you from your work. We can talk about it later."

"Nonsense," he says. "I always have time for a good hunting story. So tell me, what did you bag? A fox? A few deer?"

When neither of us respond, he says, "A hare? A squirrel?"

Elkin says, "We almost had a squirrel, but then it got away."

Father frowns, and I worry he will suggest I not return to the forest, but then a grin covers his wide face and he laughs. "When I was a youth, I did not catch anything until my fourth venture! Do not worry, it will happen."

"Thank you, Father," I say, my shoulders relaxing.

"Yes, thank you, uncle," Elkin says. "We will keep trying."

Father turns to greet his guests, and Andrew and the other page follow. As he passes me, Andrew whispers, "I shall meet you in your chambers as soon as I can free myself."

"Do hurry," I whisper back. "I shall need your help."

I turn to Elkin, but he is not there. I catch sight of him turning the corner to go up to our bedchambers. I meet him on the stairs. "If I did not know better," I say with a smile, "I would think you are trying to get away from me."

"I am," he snaps, and hurries his pace.

"But why?" I ask. "Don't you want to hear what happened to me?"

"I have to wait until *Andrew* is available, remember?"

"I just didn't want to tell it twice! It's a long story!"

We have reached the top of the stairs. Our bedchambers are in opposite directions from here. Without hesitation, he walks toward his. I follow.

"Look," he says, stopping in front of the heavy oak door, "I am tired of always coming second to Andrew. It has been this way since he arrived when we were young. I am sure the two of you can do just fine on your own."

I am stunned. "But . . . but you were always horrid to me. I thought you hated me. I befriended Andrew because he actually seemed to *like* me!"

"Perhaps I was horrid because I was lonely. Every time I came to visit, you ignored me."

"That is not the way I recall the chain of events."

"Well, I do."

"Well, I do not."

We cross our arms and glare at each other. "So what do we do now?" I ask, breaking the staring contest. "We are not children anymore. We have hunted for treasure together and discovered wondrous things. Surely we can get past this."

Elkin sighs. "I suppose so. I am sure that would be the opinion of the hermit as well. And he is very wise."

I put out my hand. "Shake?"

We shake once and at the same time both do a head-bob. This inevitably leads to us conking our heads. "Ow!" we say at the same time, then break up laughing.

"That is the second time today I have been hit on my head," I tell him. "Come to my chambers and let me give you the story."

We walk back down the hall, both rubbing our heads. I

still feel the bump from Rapunzel's attack. Andrew is pacing back and forth in front of my door.

"I would have burst if I had to wait for you any longer!" Andrew says as I open the door and the three of us pour into my room. I shut the door behind us and gesture them as far away from it as possible. I do not want anyone to overhear.

They listen avidly as I tell the story of finding Rapunzel. They laugh at the part with the bowl, and look somber when I tell of what the witch did to her family and how she is kept prisoner in that tiny room. I finish by telling them Rapunzel's plan, and ask them to help me find the silk. Elkin has proven excellent at providing cover, so he is to stand guard outside the seamstress's workroom. Part of Andrew's training is to know one fabric from another, so he is in charge of showing me which pieces of material I am to steal.

I ask Andrew where Mum is. I have not seen her since our return. The pages are the eyes and ears of this place.

"The last time I saw her was a few hours ago way down by the storage cellars," he says. "Annabelle had led her into a game of hide-and-seek. Apparently that little sister of yours is a good hider, because your mother and half the servants went off to look for her."

I smile. "I know where she is. She has lured me into that game, too. I always find her in the same place."

"Where would that be?" Andrew asks.

"Right here," I announce, throwing open the door to my wardrobe closet. Sure enough, curled up on top of my winter traveling cloak is Annabelle, sound asleep and sucking her thumb.

NIGHT

Most everyone in the castle is now asleep except for the few servants and guards on the night watch. We are creeping along the hallway with only the light of Andrew's small oil lamp to guide us. It is very quiet and dark in this part of the castle at night, since no one usually has the need to be here. We reach the seamstress's workroom and Elkin takes up his post. I slowly push the door open, grimacing as the wood scrapes against the stone floor. Andrew leads the way in, and we head directly to the shelves in the back. Long rolls of material line the shelves, and in the dark it is hard to tell what anything is.

"We are going to have to judge by feel," Andrew whispers, reaching out his hand and unfurling the ends of one of the rolls before going on to the next.

I start on a different shelf, rubbing one material after the other between my fingers. I can recognize the rough ones like wool or leather, but the rest feel the same to me.

"We don't have time for this," I tell him. "Just pick one that you think is strong enough, and let's get out of here."

"Okay, okay," he says, hurriedly testing two or three by yanking on them in both directions. "I think this is the right one." He pulls at a roll, and I help him bring it down from the shelf.

"We should only take what we need so that no one gets suspicious," I tell him.

He picks up the lamp and shines it around the room. I follow him to a table with some cutting shears. Starting at opposite ends, we cut the material into thick strips until I think we have enough to cover the distance. I put the rest of the roll away and we hurry to rejoin Elkin, who is sitting outside the doorway, sound asleep! Andrew closes the door behind us, and Elkin wakes up with a start. "Mommy?" he says, rubbing his eyes. "Have you come to tuck me in?"

Andrew and I have to stuff our fists in our mouths to keep from screaming with laughter and waking the whole castle.

CHAPTER FORTY

Rapunzel

18ᵗʰ of Augustus

When the witch comes this morning, I have to remind myself to look downcast and despondent. It isn't too hard, considering all the practice I have gotten this past fortnight. Usually she leaves as soon as she brings my food, but of course she chooses today to hang around. She has one of those huge flying bugs circling her hair, the first I have seen of them since that day in Father's garden. It makes me think of Steven and how I hope he made it to a secure hiding place.

I am hungry so, not knowing what else to do, I start eating the potatoes and beets that she brought me. She watches me eat, seemingly fascinated. I glance up for a second and I swear her wart wobbles of its own accord. I think I may toss up my food. I keep my head down after that.

Eventually she speaks. "I do not blame you for what you and that . . . that underground cave creature tried to do. I understand why you wanted to escape."

I do not respond.

"You might think that life is better out there, but you are

wrong. I know what is best for a growing girl. You will learn that I am right."

It takes all my willpower not to scream that I will not be learning ANYTHING from her, because soon enough I shall never be laying eyes on her again. She finally leaves, and I hurry to tidy up the place before the prince comes. There is not much to tidy. I push the chair under the table and straighten the blanket on the "bed." I tuck in the wisps of hair that have come loose from the braid. My scrapes have all healed, and I am pimple free. There is nothing I can do about the sorry state of my dress, though. I will be leaving the trunk behind, so I pull out the few things I will bring with me — the spoon and, even though it is nearly ruined, the shawl Mother knitted for me. Sir Kitty will be coming, too, of course. The rest the witch is welcome to.

Finally I hear the call from below and hurry to the window. I pray it is not the witch returned to tell me again that she knows what is best for me. Thankfully, it is the prince! He reaches into his satchel and holds up a big pile of purple silk.

I grin down at him and toss out the braid. He climbs faster this time, but he is still much slower than the witch.

"Was it any problem getting the silk?" I ask him when he climbs in.

He shakes his head and smiles. "Nah. I've got people on the inside." He turns the satchel upside down, and we both get busy tying the ends together to make one long rope. It moves quickly, and when we are done, he asks, "Shall we test it?"

I nod and we go to the window. The prince ties one end to the old hinge and lets the rest drop. We both squeeze into the window frame to watch.

"Huh," he says.

"Hmm," I say.

"Not quite long enough, is it?"

I shake my head. "I think it would've been, had we not needed to tie all those knots."

"I think you're right. I had not taken that into consideration. I shall get the rest tonight, and we leave tomorrow for certain. I'll take this piece with me and finish the job at the castle."

I nod and tell him that will be wonderful, but truly I want to cry. "Will you take Sir Kitty back with you today as well? Then at least I'll know she is safe."

"Of course," he says. I can tell he feels bad, too.

I pick Sir Kitty up from where she has been sunning herself on the floor and kiss her on the nose. "Don't stir up any trouble in the castle, Sir Kitty. These are good people."

She puts her paw on my chin and I feel like crying again. Before I embarrass myself further, I hand the cat to Prince Benjamin and he puts her gently into his now empty satchel and secures it over his chest.

"Do not worry," he says as I lower my hair for his descent. "You shall see her before you know it."

I nod, unable to trust myself not to burst into tears if I say anything further.

CHAPTER FORTY-ONE

Prince Benjamin

18th of Augustus

Elkin has promised to stay awake this time. Just to be sure, we have instructed him to stand with one leg raised at all times. That should keep him focused. I feel very stupid for not considering how much the silk ladder would shrink once the pieces were tied together. It barely reached halfway to the ground. Rapunzel put on a brave face, but I know she was disappointed. I have set up Sir Kitty in the royal pet room, where she will get cared for and fed at all hours of the day and night. I told the royal animal handler that I am watching her for a friend and to keep a special eye on her. He bowed and asked no questions. I gave him an excellent head-bob, if I do say so myself.

Andrew is grabbing at the rolls of material, muttering, "Where is it? It was right here last night!"

I hold the lamp up so he can see better. The purple roll is definitely not on the shelf where I stashed it. "You'll have to search on your own," I tell him. "I have to get down to the sitting room to meet Mum. Do you know what she wants to talk to me about?"

Andrew shakes his head. "You go on — I'll find it."

I hurry out, saluting Elkin as I pass him. Good to his word, he is balancing on one leg. I run through the castle to the sitting room. Mum is waiting in front of the fire, her knitting needles flashing so quickly, my eye can barely follow. Annabelle is spinning a top at her feet. Does the child not have a bedtime?

"Have a seat, Benjamin," Mum says, gesturing with her elbow to the seat beside her.

Could she have found out about my trips to the tower? I do not see how. Something is going on, though. She rarely asks to speak to me in such a formal manner. "Is something troubling you, Mum?" I ask.

She shakes her head. "Quite the opposite. I have good news. You are now engaged to be married, Benjamin. We have selected your future bride, a lovely princess who lives three kingdoms away. The wedding will take place on your seventeenth birthday."

Annabelle pops her head up and squeals, "I engaged, too, Benjy! We bof engaged!"

I should be stunned by this news. Flabbergasted and appalled. However, I have just noticed the beautiful purple silk robe that Mum is wearing.

"May I be excused?" I ask her.

She nods.

I jump out of the chair and run back down the twisting hallways to the workroom. In my brief absence, Elkin has switched to the other foot. Andrew has made a mess of the place and is still muttering to himself. "No silk, no silk anywhere!"

"You can stop your search," I announce. "Mum is WEARING it! Oh, and I am now engaged."

At that, Elkin comes running into the room, and Andrew hurries over to me, knocking aside one of the dressmaker's mannequins.

"You are *engaged*?" Elkin asks, eyes wide.

Hearing him say it, Mum's words finally sink in. "I am engaged," I repeat, sinking to my knees. "How can I be engaged? I just met the first girl I have ever liked."

LATER EVENING

I refuse to focus on Mum's announcement. I cannot let it distract me from the issue at hand. I must get that robe. I cannot let Rapunzel down again. I make Elkin and Andrew take an oath not to mention the engagement either to me or amongst themselves.

"Our goal tonight is to get that robe. Mum will be going to sleep soon, and then we shall have to whisk it from her room."

"Can't we just use another piece of fabric?" Elkin asks.

Andrew shakes his head. "Nothing else is strong enough. The next shipment is not in for a week."

Two hours later, Mum is finally snoring in her bed. Father is downstairs in his throne room arguing with his bailiff over some kingly matter involving a goat and a stash of potatoes. Mum's lady-in-waiting, Cassandra, has settled into her room next door. Unless she is kept occupied, she will certainly hear us. "You're on, Andrew," I tell him, pushing him down the hall after her.

"But what if Cassandra doesn't want to talk to me?"

"She has fancied you for years," I assure him. "Just whisper sweet nothings for five minutes."

"Fine," Andrew says grudgingly. "But you owe me."

"You can be the ring bearer at his wedding!" Elkin calls softly after him.

I give him a little shove. "You promised!"

"Sorry," he says sheepishly. "I could not resist."

I point to his left leg. He rolls his eyes but lifts his leg as he moves to his post at the side of the door. Luckily Mum's door is well oiled and opens silently. The glow of the lamp on the wall is enough to light my way. I scan the room, and do not see it at first. The door to her wardrobe is open and there must be twenty identical-looking robes hanging on wooden hangers. I pick out the new one and silently slip it off the hanger and over my shoulder. Then right before I turn to go, I grab the hanger. There is a better chance that she'll notice its absence if she sees an empty hanger. The other hangers bump into one another as I pull it out and I hold my breath. Mum's snoring remains steady so I tiptoe from the room, glad that I listened to Andrew and took off my heavy boots.

Tomorrow I will finish the job of rescuing Rapunzel, and will tell Mum that I am not marrying the princess from three kingdoms away.

Well, I'm sure I can do the first part. The second part will take more courage.

CHAPTER FORTY-TWO

Rapunzel
19th of Augustus

Up before dawn, I am counting the seconds until the witch calls to me from below. The sooner she arrives, the sooner she will leave. Then Prince Benjamin will arrive to TAKE ME OUT OF THIS PLACE.

It seems like time is moving backward this morning. If I did not know better, I would say even the blackbirds are circling just a little bit slower than usual. Finally the witch calls out, "Rapunzel, Rapunzel, let down your hair," for what will be the last time. I cannot lower my hair fast enough. It seems to take her forever to reach the top.

She has only one leg over the window ledge when I cannot help but mutter, "Honestly, you'd think you were the prince, it took you so long."

She stops climbing. If I thought time was going slowly before, now it has certainly stopped. I cannot breathe. Did I truly say that out loud? After what feels like an eternity, the witch climbs the rest of the way in and sets the bowl of food on the table. I am still holding my breath. Perhaps she did not hear me? Or thought I said something else?

No such luck. In a flash, she grabs my shoulders. I have seen her angry before, but nothing like this. Her frizzled hair stands on end, and her eyes practically bug out of her face. I am too angry with myself to be scared.

"You want to see what life is like on your own so badly? Well, here is your chance."

For a second I think she is going to just let me go. But no. She whips out a pair of shears, which makes me wonder what else she's got stored in that long black coat of hers. She yanks my braid in though the window until it is coiled at my feet. Then she turns me around so she is directly behind me. I hear the blades of the shears open, and in one cut, she snips off my entire braid and walks toward the window with it. At first I am stunned, then my hands fly up to my head. I can feel the air on the back of my neck for the first time since I was a small babe. I feel so much lighter.

I don't have any time to enjoy the new feeling, however. The witch drags me to the window, and I see she has tied my braid to the hinge. She grabs me under her arm the same way she did when she took me from my home originally. Then she climbs out the window, with me still under her arm. We slide down the braid. If I were not already my own worst enemy, I would be hitting myself right now. I cannot BELIEVE that I did not think of cutting off my braid and escaping this way. I could have just told the prince to bring me a pair of shears instead of trying to make a silk ladder, and I would have been home by now. I may be too stupid to live. Perhaps my parents were right to trade me.

The witch undoes the harness of a horse on her carriage. She throws herself onto its bare back and lifts me up in front of her. She holds me so tight, I cannot breathe. We wind in and out of trees, across brooks, and over fallen logs until I have completely lost my way. By the time we stop, I am ready to fall over.

She lifts me off the horse and tosses me (TOSSES ME!) into the middle of a circle of tall bushes. "Good luck making it through the night," she says, and takes off without a backward glance.

On my knees on the damp grass, I do not know what to feel. All my hopes dashed yet again. I look around me. The bushes are thick with thorns. The overhanging branches of the trees provide good protection from the heat of the morning sun, but I know they will also make it very cold at night. I am quite hidden in here. I am ever so thankful the prince took Sir Kitty. She would be so scared in this place.

I gasp aloud. The prince! He is going to show up at the tower and I will not be there! He will never know what has become of me. He will think I have spurned his kindness and left! Perhaps I dreamed the whole thing and there never was a prince. Or a cat. Perhaps the witch put a spell on me to make me believe all those things. My strength has fully left me and the hunger floods in. I crawl over to the nearest bush and pluck a handful of berries. I chew them listlessly, then curl up in a tight ball and try to pretend today never happened.

MIDDAY

I have tried all day, but I cannot sleep out here on the forest floor. It is altogether different down here from what I had imagined from the tower window. First off, it is noisy. Bugs and birds and animals making all sorts of squawks and calls and yelps. It is wet from the dew that gets trapped by the tree cover. I have been bitten at least three times, and stung at least once. I stand up to stretch my legs, and the ease with which I stand surprises me. Something is different. My hair! I have not had a chance to think about what the witch did. She finally gave me my birthday haircut! How long ago my birthday seems now. I am so much older now than I was then, and this short hair suits me.

I take stock of the situation. I have nothing but berries to eat, and nothing but whatever dew I can collect on the leaves that carpet the forest floor. If I tried to squeeze through the prickly bushes, I would eventually reach the other side, but I would be bloodied up quite badly. Even my limited schooling taught me that blood draws animals. At least, I am somewhat protected from them inside the circle.

I close my eyes and take a long, deep breath. I am done planning. What will happen will happen. I should have trusted Steven's words all along. I can do only one thing now.

I can sing.

CHAPTER FORTY-THREE

Prince Benjamin

19th of Augustus

I ride Snowflake right up to the base of the tower and hop off. I grab my satchel and call up, "Rapunzel, Rapunzel, let down your hair." Then to be clever I add, "So I can get you out of there!" Ah, good poetry never goes out of style.

Rapunzel lowers her braid and I climb up faster this time than before. It figures: I find the one physical activity I am not half bad at, and this will be the last time I ever do it. I hop in the window and can't wait to show her the ladder that I finished in the wee hours of the morn. But there is no girl at the end of the braid. There is only an ugly, angry, scary witch. I frantically search the room, but Rapunzel is nowhere in sight.

"What have you done with her?" I demand. I stand straight and tall and give her my most royal glare. She is not impressed. With one swing of her arm, she knocks me clear to the wall. My ears ring from the blow, and my glasses are knocked all the way across the room.

"Do you think that just because you are a prince you can do whatever you like?"

Her words sound fuzzy to me. All I can hear are *prince* and *whatever*. Do I nod or shake my head? I do not know what will bring her wrath. Nodding is the easier solution because my chin is already resting on my chest from the blow. So I lift it slightly and nod once. That apparently was the wrong answer, because the next thing I know, I am flying through the air. The witch has tossed me out the window!

I grab blindly for the braid as I fall, but when I catch hold of it, the force rips it from the hinge and it falls right along with me. It is true what they say about your life passing before your eyes when you are about to die. There I am at two, taking my first steps across the Great Lawn (I was a late bloomer). There I am at seven at my birthday party. I choose Andrew to sit next to me, instead of Elkin. Interesting. Perhaps Elkin was right and I did not treat him well. I shall have to apologize. In the next life, that is. There I am at ten, the day the midwife showed me Annabelle for the first time and she grabbed my thumb and wouldn't let go. And finally, there is Rapunzel with her glowing eyes and bright smile. My last thought shall be of her, and how I have let her down.

I fully expect to break my back as I hit the ground, but to my astonishment, I find myself upright in my saddle. I cannot believe it! Snowflake has broken my fall! The witch is screaming something from the window, but it just sounds like noise to my ears. I can make out Snowflake's neck, but without my glasses, I might as well have my eyes closed. "It is up to you, old friend, to take us home. It would probably be a good idea to move quickly before the witch decides to put a curse on us."

I drop the reins and hold on tight to his neck. I close my eyes and Snowflake takes off at a gallop. Hours pass. I spend the time imagining that Rapunzel returned to her family this morning and has forgotten all about the prince who let her down. The forest seems so quiet, but I know that is because of my damaged ears. Snowflake stops for water and I join him at the brook. I splash some on my face and neck. Nothing looks familiar, but then again, everything is a blur, anyway. I have to trust that Snowflake knows what he's doing. What choice do I have?

DUSK

Although the sun has not fully set, there is no light left in the forest. Surely we should have been back at the castle by now. My ears have cleared considerably and the croaking of the bullfrogs has joined the howling of the wolves. I might as well have died from the fall, since the wolves will soon be upon us.

We trudge ever onward, farther into the forest. I am

about to reconsider the wisdom of letting the horse lead the way when I hear something that does not sound like either croaking or howling. It almost sounds like a ditty I once heard when Father took me to an alehouse with some of the barons. I listen as hard as I can. The sound is getting closer. It is definitely that song!

Oh, she was a lovely lass, don't ya know,
With a round plump face and a rosy glow,
And wherever she went the gents went, too,
For she always said, why marry one when you can marry a few?

Rapunzel! I would recognize that voice anywhere! But how could she be here, in the middle of nowhere?

"Rapunzel!" I call out. "Can you hear me?"

The song stops. "Prince Benjamin? Is it truly you?"

"Where are you? I cannot see anything."

"I am in a ring of tall bushes. Do you see them?"

"The witch broke my glasses. I can see nothing."

She doesn't respond for a moment. When she does, there is a catch in her voice. "She found you, then. I am so sorry. It was my mistake that led to all this."

I continue to let Snowflake lead the way. He must have been drawn by Rapunzel's voice this whole time. We were never headed toward the castle at all. With more confidence than I feel, I proclaim, "Fret no more, Lady Rapunzel, for I am here to rescue you. Again. But I mean it this time."

She laughs. It sounds like music. I really AM getting soft, as Elkin said!

"I see you!" she says excitedly. "I can see your head above the bushes. I cannot come to you, because the bushes are full of prickles and we can't risk drawing blood."

"I shall toss my cloak over to you. If you lay it over the lowest bush, would that cushion your climb well enough?"

"I think so!" Rapunzel says. "Have Snowflake move a few feet to his left."

I follow her instruction and then toss the cloak up to the top of the bush. It takes a few tries before it does not simply fall back on my head. "Do you have it?" I call out.

"Yes!" she replies. "I've got the end of it."

"Start climbing," I tell her. "I shall hold on to the end that is hanging over on my side so that it doesn't slip out from under you." I find the ends fairly easily, with only a puncture or two to speak of. Then I dismount and stand at Snowflake's side.

"When you reach the top of the bush, you can slide down the cloak and Snowflake will be right there."

"I'm on the top," she says gleefully. "I see you and Snowflake now."

"Be careful," I warn her. "Go slow so you don't fall through."

A minute later she has landed in the saddle with a quiet plop. She hugs the horse's neck and then jumps down and hugs me. A girl is hugging me! What can a boy do besides hug her back?

She pulls away. "I have something for you," she says. "Hold out your hand."

I do as she says. Is she going to give me a berry? That would be nice and refreshing, but we really should be hurrying back. I can only imagine the insanity at the castle right now. But she doesn't give me a berry. She places a pair of glasses in my hands. MY glasses! I put them on my face, and the world suddenly comes into focus. I can see by the moonlight all the things Rapunzel was describing.

"Where? How? When?" I stumble over my words.

She laughs. "You left them in the tower on your first visit after you, er, *fell* and they broke. I had them tied around my neck like a necklace so the witch wouldn't see them. I bent the stems back into place for you. At the rate you break your glasses, you should have a spectacle maker on the castle premises full time!"

Now it is my turn to hug her. "You are so right! I shall appoint an official spectacle maker as soon as we return. I know just the one!" I could singlehandedly keep Other

Benjamin's father in business year-round! I am certainly old enough to appoint officials now. I could have simply done that in the first place. Of course, then I would not have wound up on the treasure hunt, and I would not have rescued Rapunzel.

Or has she rescued me?

CHAPTER FORTY-FOUR

Rapunzel
19th of Augustus

A weary Snowflake finally leads us out of the woods. In the distance I see a huge castle. It is blazing with lights. It looks more like midday here than midnight. To get to the castle, we have to pass across a huge lawn. A group of men on horseback are gathered in a circle. One of them catches sight of us and gallops over at top speed. As he gets closer, I see he has a crown on his head. I know I'm supposed to bow to a king, but can one do that on a horse?

"Benjamin!" he says in a booming voice full of love. "Rapunzel! Thank goodness you are both safe!"

Did he just say my name? I lean forward in the saddle and whisper, "How does he know my name?"

Benjamin shakes his head. "I have no idea, I swear."

The king alights from his horse, and we dismount as well. He gives the prince a long hug to the point where I doubt the boy can breathe. A woman comes running across the lawn, holding up the ends of her long dress, and practically throws herself at him as well, sobbing. The prince's face reddens and he finally disentangles himself.

"Mum, Father, this is my friend Rapunzel. She was trapped in a —"

"In a tower," his mother finishes. "Yes, yes, we know all about it."

"But how?" the prince asks. "The only people who knew about her were . . ." he trails off. "Right. I should have known. Elkin!"

"Do not blame him, son," his father says. "When you did not return, he went to look for you. When he saw your markings and found the tower abandoned and a screaming witch inside, he hurried back to alert us. Between Andrew and him, we learned the whole story. Elkin led the castle guards back there and boarded up the place for good — with the witch inside. She will never bewitch anyone again."

"You trapped the witch in the tower?" I ask the prince in awe. "You are truly brilliant."

He blushes again and kicks up a little dirt with his toe. "It was an accident, really. Just some good luck for a change."

I have embarrassed him with my compliment, but his mother beams and turns to give me a closer look. "You must be exhausted, child. Come to the castle and let us fix you a warm meal. We have sent a courier to your parents' house. He will bring them back here in the morning."

I am too happy for words right now. I let her lead me through the castle gate and into the Great Hall, where a huge feast is hurriedly being laid. Word of our return must have traveled fast. I see roast pheasant and turnips and a pig glazed with honey. My mouth waters.

Two boys around the prince's age come bounding into the room and throw their arms around him. The red-haired one I know to be Elkin, and I figure the other can be no other than Andrew the page. When they are done with the hugging and merrymaking, Andrew comes over to me and, bowing slightly, says, "I believe this is yours, Lady Rapunzel." He steps aside and I see Sir Kitty behind him, happily chasing a mouse. I was about to tell him I am not of noble blood and therefore do not deserve the title of lady, but I am too happy to see Sir Kitty. I sweep her up into my arms and twirl around singing the "Dipsy Doodle" song. (In my defense, I am truly a bit loopy from what has been the craziest day of all the crazy days). After a while, I realize everyone in the room is watching me. I stop twirling and singing, and bow clumsily. The prince starts clapping and everyone else joins in. He pulls out a chair for me and I gratefully sit.

Serving maids dish out helping after helping of everything on the table until I cannot eat even one more kernel of corn. Sir Kitty is enjoying all the scraps that wind up on the floor, and she is not alone. There are dogs, cats, mice, and I think I even see a hare or two. At one point, I could have sworn Benjamin was peeking under the table and talking to one of them, but I must have imagined it. Why would he be talking to a hare?

CHAPTER FORTY-FIVE

Prince Benjamin

20th of Augustus

It is wonderful having Rapunzel safe in the castle. Mum herself showed her to the room where she'll be staying, and I heard the squeal from down the hall when Rapunzel laid eyes on the soft canopy bed. I know it was Andrew's investigative skills that led my parents to send the courier to her parents' house. I am truly lucky to have such friends as these. The only thing that dampens my spirits is having to tell Rapunzel about my engagement. She may not care at all, but I sort of hope she does.

I do not recall my head hitting the pillow. The next thing I know, I am awakened by singing. But the song is not "The Lovely Lass," and the voice is not Rapunzel's. In fact, it is not even female. I open my eyes to see the sun well risen. Where is the singing coming from?

I follow the sounds and am led to my window. I push apart the drapes and see what must be fifty boys between ages nine and twelve. The only one I recognize is Other

Benjamin. He is leading the crowd. These must be all the *other* Other Benjamins! When they see me, they sing even louder:

Prince Benjamin, he is truly great
He saved the girl, left the witch to her fate!
Prince Benjamin, there is no match.
Prince Benjamin, rah rah!

I finally have a song written about me! Okay, so it's not the world's best song, but it's the thought that counts. I wave down to them and they wave back. Mum walks into my room and smiles when she sees the boys. They bow when they catch sight of her and slowly start to dissipate back through the fields.

"That was lovely of them," she says as I beam. "I wanted to come up before breakfast to talk to you."

"What is it? Is anything wrong?" I notice that the bandage on her hand is gone and there is only the slightest pink flush left.

She shakes her head. "I want to tell you I am proud of you for the bravery you showed rescuing Rapunzel. I am not happy that you went behind our backs, but I understand your reasons. Under the circumstances, I feel that it would not be right to ask you to marry someone you do not know. It is going against tradition, but I feel strongly that you deserve to make your own choice when the time is right."

I throw my arms around her like I used to when I was a little boy. "Thank you, Mum! Thank you!"

"All right, all right," she says, pulling me off and laughing. "Just get dressed and come down. Rapunzel's parents should be here any moment."

Joyfully I wash my face and put on my most comfortable clothes. After being in those constricting riding and hunting outfits for the past few days, it is a relief to be back in my regular clothes. When I get downstairs, I find everyone is sharing my merry mood. Mum has invited many of the neighboring lords and ladies, and they are already feasting at the table. Or perhaps they never left from last night! Jugglers are juggling real apples this time, and children are running around with streamers trailing after them. I wave at Rapunzel, who is dressed in a new green gown, her newly shortened hair clean and brushed. She looks like a different person from the girl with the frightened eyes and the dusty dress. Two ladies-in-waiting sit on either side of her, so I have to sit a few seats down.

Before I fill my belly, I ask one of the stewards to get me a piece of parchment and a quill. I write my first official letter of appointment and ask the steward to pass it to a courier.

I tell him to be sure he delivers it to the dung heap cleaner in the village. The steward seems surprised, but bows and takes his leave. I give the head-bob, but he is already gone and doesn't notice.

"Lovely," Elkin says, clapping appreciatively from across the table. "Much less chickenlike."

"Ha-ha," I reply, digging into my raspberry porridge. Rescuing damsels in distress builds a hearty appetite.

CHAPTER FORTY-SIX

Rapunzel

20th of Augustus

I watch Prince Benjamin (or Ben, as he has insisted I call him from now on) digging into his morning meal. He looks well rested and happy. I must look the same. The bed in my guest room last night was like a cloud. Granted, anything would have been better than what the witch threw together for me, but I could have slept on that bed for days, even without a sleeping potion to keep me there.

It is so glorious here, with the jugglers and with the colorful tapestries showing generations of Ben's family. And the nonstop food! I could smell it cooking before I came downstairs. But most of all, everyone is so welcoming. They must know I am not from noble stock, yet they treat me as one of their own because I am a friend of Ben's. I am about to take my last bite of honey cake when I hear raised voices outside the Great Hall. A courier rushes in, and fast on his heels are my parents!

I jump up and my mug of tea nearly spills into the lap of

one of the ladies-in-waiting who has been attending me. Luckily she pulls her skirts out of the way just in time.

"There she is!" Mother yells gleefully. She starts running toward my end of the table, pulling Father along. Their clothes are rumpled from the long trip, and they look exhausted, older. But their faces are glowing.

"Mother! Father!" I run to greet them and we meet in the middle in a group hug.

"Oh, my baby," Mother says, "you had your first haircut and I wasn't there for it!" Her eyes fill with tears and I hurry to assure her that, really, the haircut wasn't as special as she might imagine.

Father takes my shoulders and says, "Rapunzel, can you ever forgive us? We have been miserable since you were taken."

"Do not blame yourselves," I tell them as Mother wipes away more tears. "You were tricked by the witch as well. Mother doesn't even LIKE rampion."

"That's true," she says, sniffling. "I don't."

I finally notice that Ben and his parents are standing a few feet away, watching. I lead my parents over to them. They bow, and Ben and the king nod graciously in return. Ben looks so regal when he does that.

"This is the boy who rescued me," I tell my parents. I

expect them to either bow again or put out their hands to shake his, but instead Father envelops Ben in a bear hug! I flush with embarrassment, but Ben only laughs.

The page Andrew appears at Ben's side. "Pardon the interruption," he says, "but we have two more arrivals who would like to say hello to the prince and Rapunzel."

We turn around to see perhaps the oldest man I've ever seen, walking side by side with the greenest. It's Steven! MY Steven! At his appearance, gasps of surprise fill the room. Mothers pull their children close. But I squeal and run up to hug him. Ben and Elkin do the same with the old man. Minus the squealing, of course.

"Rapunzel," Ben says, turning to me and Steven, "this is the hermit who first sent me to find you. He said to listen for my destiny, and that's when I heard your singing."

"And this," I say proudly, turning Steven to face him, "is the man who was so kind to me in the tower. He risked his life for me."

We all shake hands in a big circle, grinning.

"How did you know to come here?" I ask Steven excitedly just as Ben and Elkin ask the same of the hermit.

The two men look at each other, and the hermit asks Steven, "Shall we tell them?"

"Tell us what?" Ben asks jovially, his hand resting on the old hermit's shoulder.

"Well," the hermit says, "my part in the story begins the same day that these two young princes, shall we say, *visited* my home for the first time. Steven here had run past my cave earlier that day. He was ranting about a witch, and a girl locked in a tower. The poor man was terrified and miserable that he had left the girl. He made me promise that I would get help for her. He had run so far and so fast that he could not tell me how to find the tower again. I promised I would do my best, and off he went to find his family."

I can tell by their wide-eyed expressions that my parents are having a hard time taking all of this in. I reach out to take one of Mother's hands in mine, and then Father's in my other, like I used to when I was a little girl. I look up at Steven with tears in my eyes. "That was so thoughtful of you."

Steven's face turns the light purple that I know means he is embarrassed.

The hermit continues. "I did not know how to proceed. How could an old man like myself travel the Great Forest? Before long, you two fine lads showed up and, while you were in the back cave admiring my art, I heard the singing." He turns to me. "Your singing. Then the prince bemoaned the lack of adventure in his life, and I knew I had my solution. I did not tell him what I knew of the tower and the girl, for then it would not have been his story. When I heard all the castle guards thundering in the forest yesterday, I inquired what the cause was. I learned the witch had been foiled, so I went in search of Steven to let him know it was safe to come out of hiding."

"But how did he find you?" I ask Steven.

He smiles. "People who live in caves tend to know where the other cave dwellers are. It did not take him long to find someone who led him to me."

I beam at Steven. "So our escape plan worked after all! Just a little differently than we'd intended."

We laugh. Ben laughs, too, and says, "I knew it was too good to be true! Now they'll have to put both of your names in the song alongside mine!"

"No, indeed," the hermit says, suddenly serious. "This story is yours, and that is how it shall remain for the rest of history."

"Far be it from me to break up the revelry," the queen says, sweeping up behind us, "but the warm parts of the meal are getting cold, and the cold parts are getting warm. The new arrivals must be famished from their journey." She ushers us over to a newly set table. As Steven takes his seat, a young boy tentatively sticks out his hand and rubs Steven's arm. Steven smiles and says, "Nope, it doesn't rub off."

The boy giggles and his mother grabs him away, apologizing.

"It's all right," Steven says. "The first time I saw one of you, I thought my eyes were playing tricks on me, too."

"Steven," I say gravely as the bowls of turtle soup are placed before us, "I tried to save your spoon, truly I did. But my trunk is still in the tower."

"On the contrary," a voice says. I look up to see Andrew behind me. "In her fury, the witch hurled your trunk at the guards below. It burst into pieces, and everything was covered in ink. But one of the guards managed to salvage a small silver spoon from the mess. I suggested it might be important to you. I believe it is waiting for you up in your room."

"Thank you, Andrew," I tell him, my eyes filling with tears as Steven squeezes my hand affectionately.

"You have found good people," Steven whispers as Andrew resumes his position a few feet away from the table.

"I know," I whisper back, stealing a glance at Ben, who catches my eye and blushes.

"While we are all gathered here," the queen says, rising from her seat, "has anyone happened to see my new purple silk robe? It has simply *disappeared* from my chambers."

Andrew slowly backs out of the room while Ben, Elkin, and I slink down in our seats. Elkin coughs and says, "Er, funny story, Aunt. You're going to laugh. . . ."

Read the latest **wish** books!

donut go breaking my heart
suzanne nelson

Graceful
WENDY MASS

angela cervantes
ALLIE, FIRST AT LAST

carolyn mackler
best friend next door

TWICE UPON A TIME
Rapunzel
The One with All the Hair
WENDY MASS

deep down popular
phoebe stone

REVENGE OF THE **ANGELS**
JENNIFER ZIEGLER

Natalie Blitt
CAROLS AND CRUSHES

Sealed with a Secret
LISA SCHROEDER